Richard H. Stoddard, Richard Henry Stoddard

Henry Wadsworth Longfellow

A medley in prose and verse

Richard H. Stoddard, Richard Henry Stoddard

Henry Wadsworth Longfellow
A medley in prose and verse

ISBN/EAN: 9783337374136

Printed in Europe, USA, Canada, Australia, Japan

Cover: Foto ©Andreas Hilbeck / pixelio.de

More available books at **www.hansebooks.com**

HENRY WADSWORTH LONGFELLOW.

A Medley

IN PROSE AND VERSE.

BY

RICHARD HENRY STODDARD.

NEW YORK:

GEORGE W. HARLAN & CO., PUBLISHERS,

44 WEST 23D STREET.

1882.

H. J. HEWITT, PRINTER, 27 ROSE STREET, NEW YORK.

ANCESTORS.

Boast not these titles of your ancestors,
Brave youths ; they're their possessions, none of yours
When your own virtues equalled have their names,
'Twill be but fair to lean upon their fames,
For they are strong supporters ; but, till then,
The greatest are but growing gentlemen.
It is a wretched thing to trust to reeds ;
What all men do, they urge not their own deeds
Up to their ancestors ; the river's side,
By which you're planted, shows your fruit shall bide ;
Hang all your rooms with one large pedigree :
'Tis virtue alone is true nobility,
Which virtue from your father, ripe, will fall ;
Study illustrious him, and you'll have all.

BEN JONSON.

'Tis poor, and not becoming perfect gentry,
To build their glories at their fathers' cost ;
But at their own expense of blood or virtue
To raise them living monuments. Our birth
Is not our own act ; honour upon trust
Our ill deeds forfeit ; and the wealthy sums
Purchas'd by others' fame or sweat will be
Our stain ; for we inherit nothing truly
But what our actions make us worthy of.

CHAPMAN AND SHIRLEY

SALVE.

The race of greatness never dies,
Here, then, its fiery children rise,
  Perform their splendid parts,
  And captive take our hearts.

Men, women of heroic mould
Have overcome us from of old;
  Crowns waited then, as now,
  For every royal brow.

The victor in the Olympian games—
His name among the proudest names
  Was handed deathless down;
  To him the olive crown.

And they, the poets, grave and sage,
Stern masters of the tragic stage,
  Who moved by art austere
  To pity, love, and fear—

To these was given the laurel crown,
Whose lightest leaf conferred renown
  That through the ages fled
  Still circles each gray head.

R. H. STODDARD.

THE PASSING-BELL.

Hark! how chimes the passing-bell.
There's no musick to a knell :
All the other sounds we hear
Flatter, and but cheat our ear.
This doth put us still in mind
That our flesh must be resign'd,
And a general silence made,
The world be muffled in a shade.
He that on his pillow lies,
Tear-embalm'd before he dies,
Carries, like a sheep, his life
To meet the sacrificer's knife,
And for Eternity is prest,
Sad bell-wether to the rest.

JAMES SHIRLEY.

BIBLIOGRAPHY OF LONGFELLOW.

I.

ELEMENTS OF FRENCH GRAMMAR. Translated from the French of C. F. L'Homond. [Boston: 1830.]

ORIGIN AND PROGRESS OF THE FRENCH LANGUAGE. *North Amer. Rev.* 32. 277. [April, 1831.]

DEFENCE OF POETRY. *North Amer. Rev.* 34. 56. [Jan., 1832.]

HISTORY OF THE ITALIAN LANGUAGE AND DIALECTS. *North Amer. Rev.* 35. 283. [October 1832.]

SYLLABUS DE LA GRAMMAIRE ITALIENNE. [Boston: 1832.]

COURS DE LANGUE FRANÇAISE. [Boston: 1832.]
  I. Le Ministre de Wakefield.
  II. Proverbes Dramatiques.

SAGGI DE' NOVELLIERI ITALIANI D'OGNI SECOLO: Tratti da' più celebri scrittori, con brevi notizie intorno alla vita di ciascheduno. [Boston: 1832.]

SPANISH DEVOTIONAL AND MORAL POETRY. *North Amer. Rev.* 34. 277. [April, 1832.]

COPLAS DE MANRIQUE. A translation from the Spanish. [Boston: Allen & Ticknor. 1833.]

SPANISH LANGUAGE AND LITERATURE. *North Amer. Rev.* 36. 316. [April, 1833.]

OLD ENGLISH ROMANCES. *North Amer. Rev.* 37. 374. [Oct., 1833.]

OUTRE-MER: a Pilgrimage beyond the Sea. 2 vols. [Harpers: 1835.]

THE GREAT METROPOLIS. *North Amer. Rev.* 44. 461. [April, 1837.]
  A lively review of a new work on London.

HAWTHORNE'S TWICE-TOLD TALES. *North Amer. Rev.* 45. 59. [July, 1837.]

TEGNÉR'S FRITHIOFSSAGA. *North Amer. Rev.* 45. 149. [July, 1837.]

ANGLO-SAXON LITERATURE. *North Amer. Rev.* 47. 90. [July, 1838.]

vii

HYPERION: a romance.   2 vols.   [New York: 1839.]
VOICES OF THE NIGHT.   [Cambridge: 1839.]
    Reviewed in *North Amer. Rev.* 50. 266–269; *Christ. Ex.* 28. 242.
THE FRENCH LANGUAGE IN ENGLAND.   *North Amer. Rev.* 51. 285.   [Oct.
    1840.]
BALLADS, AND OTHER POEMS.   [Cambridge: 1841.]
POEMS ON SLAVERY.   [1842.]
    Composed during a return voyage from Europe, in 1842.
THE SPANISH STUDENT: a play in three acts.   [1843.]
[Editor.]   THE WAIF: a collection of poems.   [Cambridge: 1845.]
[Editor.]   THE POETS AND POETRY OF EUROPE.   [Philadelphia: 1845.]
THE BELFRY OF BRUGES, and other poems.   [Boston: 1846.]
[Editor.]   THE ESTRAY: a collection of poems.   [Boston: 1847.]
EVANGELINE: a tale of Acadie.   [1847.]
KAVANAGH: a tale.   Prose.   [Boston: 1849.]
THE SEASIDE AND THE FIRESIDE.   [Boston: 1850.]
THE GOLDEN LEGEND.   [Boston: 1851.]
    Reviewed in *Blackwood*, 5. 71; in *Eclec.* 4th s. 31. 455.
THE SONG OF HIAWATHA.   [Boston: 1855.]
    Reviewed by Rev. E. E. Hale in *North Amer. Rev.* 82. 272.
THE COURTSHIP OF MILES STANDISH.   [Boston: 1858.]
    Reviewed by A. P. Peabody in *North Amer. Rev.* 88. 275.
TALES OF A WAYSIDE INN.   [Boston: 1863.]
FLOWER DE LUCE.   [Boston: 1867.]   12 poems.
NEW ENGLAND TRAGEDIES.   [Boston: 1868.]
    I.   John Endicott.
    II.   Giles Cory of the Salem Farms.
    Reviewed by E. J. Cutler in *North Amer. Rev.* 108. 669.
DANTE'S DIVINA COMMEDIA.   A translation.   [Boston: 1867–70.]
    Three vols.   I. Inferno.   II. Purgatorio.   III. Paradiso.   The same
    in one vol.
    Reviewed by Charles Eliot Norton in *North Amer. Rev.* 105. 125;
    by George W. Greene in *Atlantic M.* 20. 188.
THE DIVINE TRAGEDY.   [Boston: 1872.]
CHRISTUS: A MYSTERY.   [Boston: 1872.]
    Collecting, for the first time, into their consecutive unity:
    I.   The Divine Tragedy.
    II.   The Golden Legend.
    III.   The New England Tragedies.

THREE BOOKS OF SONG. [Boston: 1872.]
AFTERMATH. [Boston: 1874.]
THE MASQUE OF PANDORA, and other poems. [Boston: 1875.]
[Editor.] POEMS OF PLACES. 31 vols. [Boston: 1876–1879.]
KERAMOS, and other poems. [Boston: 1878.]
ULTIMA THULE. [Boston: 1880.]
THE POETICAL WORKS OF HENRY WADSWORTH LONGFELLOW. Containing
a superb new steel portrait by Wm. E. Marshall, and illustrated
by more than six hundred wood-engravings, designed especially
for this work by the best American artists. [Houghton, Mifflin
& Co. : 1881.]

II.

ADDITIONAL NOTICES OF MR. LONGFELLOW.

ARNAUD, Simon. *La Légende Dorée.* [In *Le Correspondant :* 10
Juillet, 1872.]
COBB, J. B. Miscellanies. [1858.] pp. 330–357.
CURTIS, G. W. *Atlantic Monthly,* 12. 269.
Mr. Curtis's "Easy Chair" in *Harper's Monthly* contains notices of
Mr. Longfellow and his writings, as follows : the "Dante," 35.
257 ; "Reception in England," 37. 561 ; "New England Tra-
gedies," 38. 271 : "The Divine Tragedy," 44. 616. There is
also a general article on Longfellow in 1. 74.
COCHIN, Augustin. *La Poésie en Amérique.* [In *Le Correspondant :*
10 Juillet, 1872.]
DEPRET, Louis. *Le Va-et-Vient.* [Paris : n. d.]
The Same. *La Poésie en Amérique.* [Lille : 1876.]
DE PRINS, A. *Études Américaines.* [Louvain : 1877.]
FRISWELL, J. H. *Modern Men of Letters.* [1870.] pp. 285-99.
GILFILLAN, George. *Literary Portraits.* Second Series. [1849.]
PALMER, Ray. Longfellow and his Works. *Int. Rev.* [Nov., 1875.]
PECK, G. W. Review of Mr. Longfellow's *Evangeline.* [New York :
1848.]
P. T. C. *Kalevala and Hiawatha.* A review. [185-.] pp. 21.
WHIPPLE, E. P. *Essays and Reviews.* 1. 60-61-62-63.

III.

TRANSLATIONS OF MR. LONGFELLOW'S WORKS.

ENGLISH.

Noel. [A French poem by Longfellow in *Flower de Luce.*] Tr. by J. E. Norcross. [Philadelphia : 1867. Large paper. 50 copies printed.]

GERMAN.

Englische Gedichte aus Neuerer Zeit. Freiligrath, Ferdinand. . . . H. W. Longfellow. . . . [Stuttgardt und Tübingen : 1846.]

Longfellow's Gedichte. Übersetzt von Carl Böttger. [Dessau : 1856.]

Balladen und Lieder von H. W. Longfellow. Deutsch von A. R. Nielo. [Münster : 1857.]

Longfellow's Gedichte. Von Friedrich Marx. [Hamburg und Leipzig: 1868.]

Longfellow's ältere und neuere Gedichte in Auswald. Deutsch von Adolf Laun. [Oldenburg : 1879.]

Der Spanische Studente. Übersetzt von Karl Böttger. [Dessau : 1854.]

The Same. Von Maria Helene Le Maistre. [Dresden : n. d.]

The Same. Übersetzt von Häfeli. [Leipzig : n. d.]

Evangeline. Aus dem Englischen. [Hamburg : 1857.]

The Same. Aus dem Englischen, von P. J. Belke. [Leipzig : 1854.]

The Same. Eine Erzählung aus Acadien. Von Eduard Nickles. [Karlsruhe : 1862.]

The Same. Übersetzt von Frank Siller. [Milwaukee : 1879.]

The Same. Übersetzt von Karl Knortz. [Leipzig : n. d.]

Longfellow's Evangeline. Deutsch von Heinrich Vichoff. [Trier : 1869.]

Die Goldene Legende. Deutsch von Karl Keck. [Wien : 1859.]

The Same. Übersetzt von Elise Freifrau von Hohenhausen. [Leipzig: 1880.]

Das Lied von Hiawatha. Deutsch von Adolph Böttger. [Leipzig : 1856.]

Der Sang von Hiawatha. Übersetzt von Ferdinand Freiligrath. [Stuttgardt und Augsburg : 1857.]

Hiawatha. Übertragen von Hermann Simon. [Leipzig : n. d]
Der Sang von Hiawatha. Übersetzt, eingeleitet und erklärt von Karl
Knortz. [Jena : 1872.]
Miles Standish's Brautwerbung. Aus dem Englischen von F. E.
Baumgarten. [St. Louis : 1859.]
Die Brautwerbung des Miles Standish. Übersetzt von Karl Knortz.
[Leipzig : 18—.]
Miles Standish's Brautwerbung. Übersetzt von F. Manefeld. [1867.]
Die Sage von König Olaf. Übersetzt von Ernst Rauscher.
The Same. Übersetzt von W. Hertzberg.
Dorfschmid. Die Alte Uhr auf der Treppe. Des Sklaven Traum.
Tr. by H. Schmick. *Archiv. f. d. Stud. d. n. Spr.* 1858. 24. 214–
217.
Gedichte von H. W. L. Deutsch von Alexander Neidhardt. [Darm-
stadt : 1856.]
Der Bau des Schiffes. Tr. by Th. Zermelo. *Archiv. f. d. Stud. d. n.
Spr.* 1861. 30. 293–304.
Hyperion. Deutsch von Adolph Böttger. [Leipzig : 1856.]
Ein Psalm des Lebens, etc. Deutsch von Alexander Neidhardt.
Archiv. f. d. Stud. d. n. Spr. 1856. 29. 205–203.
Die Göttliche Tragödie. Übersetzt von Karl Keck. [MS.]
The Same. Übersetzt von Hermann Simon. [MS.]
Pandora. Übersetzt von Isabella Schuchardt. [Hamburg : 1878.]
Morituri Salutamus. Übersetzt von Dr. Ernst Schmidt. [Chicago :
1878.]
The Hanging of the Crane—Das Kesselhängen. Übersetzt von G. A.
Zündt. [n. d.]
The Same. Das Einhängen des Kesselhakens, frei gearbeitet von Joh.
Henry Becker. [n. d.]

DUTCH.

Het Lied van Hiawatha. In het Nederdeutsch overgebragt door L. S.
P. Meijboom. [Amsterdam : 1862.]
Miles Standish. Nagezongen door S. I. Van den Berg. [Haarlem :
1861.]

SWEDISH.

Hyperion. På Svenska, af Grönlund. [1853.]
Evangeline. På Svenska, af Alb. Lysander. [1854.]

The Same.   Öfversatt af Iljalmar Erdgren.   [Göteborg : 1875.]
The Same.   Öfversatt af Philip Svenson.   [Chicago : 1875.]
Hiawatha.   På Svenska af Westberg.   [1856.]

DANISH.

Evangeline.   Paa Norsk ved Sd. C. Knutsen.   [Christiania: 1874.]
Sangen om Hiawatha.   Oversat af G. Bern.   [Kjöbenhavn : 1860.]

FRENCH.

Evangeline ; suivie des Voix de la Nuit.   Par le Chevalier de Chatelain.
[Jersey, London, Paris, New York : 1856.]
The Same.   Conte d'Acadie.   Traduit par Charles Brunel.   Prose.
[Paris : 1864.]
The Same.   Par Léon Pamphile Le May.   [Quebec : 1865.]
La Légende Dorée, et Poëmes sur l'Esclavage.   Traduits par Paul Blier
et Edward Mac-Donnel.   Prose.   [Paris et Valenciennes : 1854.]
Hiawatha.   Traduit de l'Anglais par M. H. Gomont.   [Nancy, Paris :
1860.]
Drames et Poésies.   Traduits par X. Marmier.   The New England
Tragedies.   [Paris: 1872.]
Hyperion et Kavanagh.   Traduit de l'Anglais, et précédé d'une Notice
sur l'auteur.   2 vols.   [Paris et Bruxelles: 1860.]
The Psalm of Life, and Other Poems.   Tr. by Lucien de la Rive in
Essais de Traduction Poétique.   [Paris: 1870.]

ITALIAN.

Alcune poesie di Enrico W. Longfellow.   Traduzione dall' Inglese di
Angelo Messedaglia.   [Padova: 1866.]
Lo Studente Spagnuolo.   Prima Versione Metrica di Messandro Baz-
zini.   [Milano: 1871.]
The Same.   Traduzione di Nazzareno Trovanelli.   [Firenze: 1876.]
Poesie sulla Schiavitù.   Tr. in versi Italiani da Louisa Grace Bartolini.
[Firenze : 1860.]
Evangelina.   Tradotta da Pietro Rotondi.   [Firenze : 1857.]
The Same.   Traduzione di Carlo Faccioli.   [Verona : 1873.]
La Leggenda d'Oro.   Tradotta da Ada Corbellini Martini.   [Parma :
1867.]

Il Canto d'Hiawatha. Tr. da L. G. Bartolini. Frammenti. [Firenze : 1867.]

Miles Standish. Traduzione dall' Inglese di Caterino Frattini. [Padova : 1868.]

PORTUGUESE.

El Rei Roberto de Sicilia. Tr. by Dom Pedro II., Emperor of Brazil. [Autograph MS.]

Evangelina. Traducida por Franklin Doria. [Rio de Janeiro : 1874.]

The Same. Poema de Henrique Longfellow. Traducido por Miguel Street de Arriaga. [Lisbon : n. d.]

The Same. By Flavio Reimar, in the *Aurora Brazileira*, 1874 ; and by José de Goes Filho, in the *Municipio*, 1874.

SPANISH.

Evangelina. Romance de la Acadia. Traducido del Ingles por Carlos Mórla Vicuña. [Nueva York : 1871.]

POLISH.

Zlota Legenda. The Golden Legend. Tr. into Polish by F. Jerzierski. [Warszawa : 1857.]

Evangelina. Tr. into Polish by Felix Jerzierski. [Warszawa : 1857.]

Duma o Hiawacie. The Song of Hiawatha. Tr. into Polish by Feliksa Jerzierskiego. [Warszawa : 1860.]

RUSSIAN AND OTHER LANGUAGES.

Excelsior, and other poems, in Russian. [St. Petersburg : n. d.]

Hiawatha, rendered into Latin, with abridgment. By Francis William Newman. [London : 1862.]

Excelsior. Tr. into Hebrew by Henry Gersoni. [n. d.]

A Psalm of Life. In Marathi. By Mrs. H. I. Bruce. [Satara : 1878.]

The Same. In Chinese. By Jung Tagen. [Written on a fan.]

The Same. In Sanscrit. By Elihu Burritt and his pupils.

There is one point in relation to the works of Longfellow which deserves especial mention. It is the frequency with which his poems have been selected by composers for musical illustration. Some of them are the following :

Operas.—" The **Masque of Pandora**," libretto arranged by Bolton Rowe, music by Alfred Cellier ; " **Victorian, the Spanish Student**," libretto by Julian Edwards, music by J. Reynolds Anderson.

Cantatas.—" The **Wreck of the Hesperus**," composed by T. Anderton ; " The **Consecration of the Banner**," by J. F. H. Read ; " The **Building of the Ship**," by J. F. Barnett, another by Henry Lahee ; " The **Golden Legend**," by Dudley Buck, another by the Rev. H. E. Hodson ; " The **Bells of Strassburg Cathedral** " (from " The Golden Legend "), by Franz Liszt ; " The **Tale of a Viking** " (" The Skeleton in Armor "), by George E. Whiting.

Two, Three, and Four-Part Songs.—" Stars of Summer Night," by Henry Smart, Dr. E. G. Monk, J. L. Hatton ; " Good-Night, Beloved," by Ciro Pinsuti, J. L. Hatton, Dr. E. G. Monk ; " Beware " (" I Know a Maiden "), by J. L. Hatton, J. B. Boucher, H. De Burgh, Mrs. Mounsey Bartholomew, M. W. Balfe ; " The Reaper and the Flowers," by J. B. Boucher, A. R. Gaul ; " Song of the Silent Land," by A. R. Gaul, A. H. D. Prendergast ; " The Curfew," by T. Anderton, P. H. Diemer, W. Macfaren, Henry Smart ; " The Day is Done," by A. R. Gaul ; " The Hemlock Tree," by J. L. Hatton ; " The Village Blacksmith," by J. L. Hatton ; " King Witlaf's Drinking-Horn," by J. L. Hatton ; " The Arrow and the Song," by Walter Hay ; " The Wreck of the Hesperus," by Dr. H. Hiles ; " A Voice came over the Sea " (" Daybreak "), by F. Quinn ; " A Psalm of Life," by Henry Smart, Dr. Mainzer ; " The Rainy Day," by A. S. Sullivan ; " Woods in Winter," by W. W. Pearson ; " Up and Doing," by Dr. Mainzer ; " Heart Within and God O'erhead," by Rossini ; " The Nun of Nidaros " and " King Olaf's Christmas," from the " Saga of King Olaf," by Dudley Buck ; the latter two being choruses for male voices, with solos. As for songs for a single voice, they are very numerous.

HENRY WADSWORTH LONGFELLOW.

I HAVE set myself a difficult task in undertaking to write and edit a Medley which shall concern itself with the life and works of Mr. Longfellow, but, having undertaken it, I purpose to go on with it to the best of my ability. About the middle of April, 1878, I resolved to spend a few weeks on the seashore of Massachusetts, and, not wishing to be entirely idle while there, I procured the complete writings of Mr. Longfellow, with the intention of making a study thereof for the pages of *Scribner's Monthly*. I was, of course, familiar with the body of his poetry and had a tolerably clear idea of his prose, but this did not satisfy me. I determined, therefore, to read the books which I was to take with me, to make notes as I read, and not write until I had reached conclusions which I was prepared to stand by. I tried to be critical: I know I was conscientious.

Before leaving town I naturally communicated with Mr. Longfellow, and in what follows I shall make some use of his answer, or answers, to my informal notes. Mr. Longfellow's first reply, which is dated at Cambridge, April 20, 1878, needs no comment :

" DEAR MR. STODDARD : In the 'Homes of American Authors,' published by Putnam of your city in 1853, you will find on page 265 a view of the house in which I was born. It is still standing, overlooking the harbor, as you see in the picture.

" Before I was two years old the family removed to a house in the centre of the town. Of this house, where my childhood was passed, I send you a photograph. The upper room in the left-hand corner, with the open windows, was mine.

"I am glad you are going to take the trouble of writing the Sketch for *Scribner*. If there is to be any biography in it, please say that the family came from Yorkshire, not from Hampshire, as usually stated ; and that my wife died at Rotterdam, and not Heidelberg.

" This is, perhaps, of no real importance, but, generally speaking, fact is better in history than fiction.

" Any other doubtful points I shall be happy to settle for you, if you will put them in the form of questions.

" You must greatly miss your friend Taylor. Still, I rejoice in his appointment. He will fill the place better than any other man.

" Yours very truly,
"HENRY W. LONGFELLOW."

The substantial facts of Mr. Longfellow's life down to the summer when I wrote were as follows: He was born on the 27th of February, 1807, at Portland, Maine. The family, as he said, came from York- shire, where the first of the name were found in 1510 living in and about Ilkley. They appear to have been sons of the soil. That is to say, they took their name from some ancestor, or town, or trade—quite likely from some ancestor whose height suggested and justified the name of Longfellow. The original Longfellow, John, a day-laborer, petitioned for a tenement which belonged, I believe, to the Middle- tons, in whose possession it still remains. He was a laborer in 1523, when he paid the price of one day's work—fourpence—to aid the King in his war with the French. Farm-hands in the beginning, and then farmers, a Longfellow in the reign of Henry VIII. was the wealthiest man in his neighborhood, and shortly before the Reformation two of the family were vicars of churches. They started in poverty, nevertheless, and so went on, handing down the bap- tismal John. There was a John William Longfellow in the third generation who had the lime-kilns of Ilkley, for which he paid a rent of twenty shillings per annum. They married daughters of the soil, buxom lasses, whose sturdy descendants still till the fertile meadows of Yorkshire. Tradition says that

they would help themselves to green yews for bows,
and would keep dogs to hunt game—misdemeanors
for which they were repeatedly fined.

It becomes me to say here that I am indebted for
what I state in regard to the ancestry of Mr. Longfellow to my good friend Robert Collyer, who has
kindly loaned me a discourse which he delivered
upon the Longfellows in England at the Messiah
on the 9th of April and which, I think, is to form
part of a future volume. He traces the Longfellow
family through its Johns and Williams until he finds
upon the old church register a William, the son of
a John, who was baptized at Ilkley on the 22d of
February, 16$\frac{34}{5}$, and whom the vicar of Ilkley believed to be the founder of the family. According
to a record among the vicar's papers, he settled in
Newbury, Massachusetts, where he married Anne
Sewall on the 10th of November, 1676, a person
of some consequence, who bore him three sons and
two daughters. He was an officer in the Essex regi-
ment, and was drowned off Cape Breton in an expedition against the French and Indians. The particu-
larity of this account would seem to authenticate it,
but it does not; for while it corresponds with the
account to which I gave currency four years ago, at
least as far as the place of settlement of this William Longfellow, the maiden name of the lady whom

he married, and his death by drowning are concerned, it does not correspond with what I believed to be the year of his birth, which I then fixed upon, 1651—an error, if it be an error, which was not perceived or not corrected by Mr. Longfellow, who did me the honor to read the proof of my Sketch.

Either I am no genealogist, which is likely, or, which is quite as likely, the genealogy of the Longfellows in America is somewhat uncertain. I have been consulting the Journals of those old-time Portland dominies, Thomas Smith and Samuel Deane, and I find in the entries of the first, under the date of April 11, 1745, "Mr. Longfellow came to live here." Then, in a note, several Longfellows are bunched together. As first, the one who went to Portland at the time specified—Stephen, who was graduated at Harvard College in 1742, and who, the son of an earlier Stephen, was born at Byfield in 1723. The first of the name in New England (the note asserts) was William, grandfather and great-grandfather of these Stephens, who married Mistress Anne Sewall in 1678 and settled at Byfield, where he became a merchant. But William is declared a little later *not* to have been the first who emigrated, but to have followed an older relative, a brother perhaps, a Stephen, who, I imagine, was from Ilkley. Another Stephen, a descendant in the third or fourth generation, married

Mistress Tabitha Blagdon, of York, in 1749, by whom he had three sons, Stephen, Samuel, and William, and a daughter Tabitha. The first of these, born in 1750, married Mistress Patience Young, of York, in December, 1777, who was the mother of another Stephen, who rose to provincial eminence. He was for about fifteen years master of a Grammar School; for twenty-five years Parish Clerk; for twenty-two years Town Clerk; for many years Clerk of the Proprietors of the Public Land; and, from the incorporation of the County in 1760 to the beginning of the Revolution in 1775, Register of the Probate and Clerk of the Judicial Courts. He died in 1790, at Gorham. His son Stephen, who was Judge of the Court of Common Pleas from 1797 to 1811, died in Gorham in 1824 at the age of seventy-four. He left a son Stephen, who was born in April, 1776, and who was graduated at Harvard in 1798. He established himself at Portland, where for forty years he was a magnate of the town. He was a member of the Hartford Convention, and afterwards, when the position was esteemed honorable, a member of Congress. He married Tabitha, a daughter of General Wadsworth, who in the fulness of time was the mother of Henry Wadsworth Longfellow. Such, as nearly as I can make it out, is the tangled genealogy of the American Longfellows. When I add to this that the early emigrant William Longfellow is reported to have been drowned at Anticosti, a large desert island in the estuary of the St. Lawrence; that the last Stephen Longfellow, besides being President of the Maine Historical Society, was a good jurist, as the Massachusetts and Maine Reports testify; and that his wife was a descendant of the valorous John Alden, as was also the mother of William Cullen Bryant, I have done with pedigrees.

The Portland to which Mr. Stephen Longfellow removed at the beginning of the present century was a town of less than four thousand inhabitants. It stood upon a little promontory fronting Casco Bay, at the eastern end of which was his mansion—an old-fashioned, wooden, two-storied dwelling, such as is common in New England, about a stone's throw from the water. It remains pretty much as it was, though it has been repaired of late years, and is now occupied by several Celtic families, whose fathers, and brothers, and sons, and cousins are employed in the Eagle Sugar House, the storehouse of which is adjoining. The country quietness which originally characterized the place still nestles in its old gardens and around the shadows of its stately elms. Besides these were trees, and vines, and flowers at the corner of Fore and Hancock Streets, where the Longfellows lived, and

there was a wilderness of greenery in the Eastern
Burying Ground, where, surrounded by the dust of
earlier generations, side by side, like brothers who
had sheathed their swords, slept the brave commanders of the *Blythe* and the *Boxer*.

The people of Portland were plain, simple folk,
seafaring traders, whose packets went to the West
Indies laden with Northern notions, and returned with rum, sugar, molasses, and other "W. I.
Goods." Craft of all sorts lay at their wharves,
and sailors of different nationalities sauntered along
their streets and alleys, singing naval ditties about
Lawrence, and Hull, and Perry. Though no par-
ticulars of the life of Master Longfellow have yet
been vouchsafed to the outer world, it is certain
from his parentage and the period wherein he lived
that he was tenderly and thoughtfully nurtured.
We may readily imagine that his good mother
taught him the alphabet; that he learned to read
out of the Bible; that he was familiar with the
hymns of Watts and Doddridge; that he was present at the morning and evening prayers of the
family; that he went to Sunday-school twice a
day, and sat drowsily through the sermon. All this
goes without saying, for it was the custom of New
England at the beginning of the century. The
church to which he was carried, or led, was doubt-

less the First Parish Meeting-House, which was
erected in 1740, and was extant nearly a century
later. It was builded after the sacred architecture
then in vogue, and was an oblong box of a building, with a tall, spire steeple, an entrance in front,
and a porch entrance upon one of its sides. Such a
church, though apparently not so large, and minus
the tall steeple, is now extant in Hingham, and it
may be accepted as a representation of the old
meeting-house at Portland. Within the pews
branched off on both sides of the aisles, and the
male and female members of the congregation were
apart by themselves. The pulpit was reached from
a platform by a staircase of polished mahogany
banisters and rungs. There was a door behind it
that opened into a chamber in which the minister
put on his robe and bands. Above it was a sound-
ing-board, and below the railed space of the altar.
A gallery ran round three sides of the house, where,
in high pews and on hard seats, sat bolt upright
the unruly urchins of the parish, under the eyes
of their theological guardians, who kept them in
order, and when they could—awake. Facing the
pulpit was the choir, the members whereof warbled
their native wood-notes wild to the music of a
bass-viol, and, it may be, the rumbling of an organ,
rising to sing as their leader struck his tuning-fork,

and following the precentor line by line. Add to
this the long prayers, the longer sermons, the passing round of the contribution-boxes, and the doxo-
logy, you have a tolerably accurate picture of the
meeting-house of our fathers.

As the Longfellow brood grew larger we may conceive of them as studying their lessons out of the
same books; doing their sums upon opposite
sides of the same slates or blackboards; reciting
in the same classes; going to and from school morning and evening with their satchels, and enjoying
the same childish games and sports. Their Wed-
nesdays and Saturdays were holidays – the latter,
however, only till sundown. We may imagine all
happy things of these rosy Longfellow children and
their companions. They are in the dusk of the
best room, where the blinds are not allowed to let
in much sunshine; they are in the garret, rummag-
ing over the faded finery of their ancestors; they
dibble in the garden in their own little plots of
ground; they pluck flowers, climb trees, tell stories,
sing, and live as if life were to be always as bright
as then, and as if (ah, that if!) there were to be no
more graves! Sometimes they strolled about the
wharves on Fore Street, and watched the sunburnt
sailors with rings in their ears,

  "Full of strange oaths, and bearded like a pard,"

hoisting out hogsheads and bales, and lowering
them on drays, and taking into their dark holds
cargoes of Yankee merchandise. Or they sat beneath the elms in the Eastern Burying Ground,
under the infinite, cloudless summer sky, and gazed
down, up, and out along the shimmering waves of
Casco Bay and its multitudinous wooded islands.
That such a childhood as I have imagined for the
young Longfellows was not entirely imaginary is
evident from one of Mr. Longfellow's poems, written in the maturity of his powers, and with the remembrance of Portland vividly before him. As a
proof of this I copy here the third stanza of "My
Lost Youth" :

> " I remember the black wharves and the slips,
> 　And the sea-tides tossing free ;
> And the Spanish sailors with bearded lips,
> And the beauty and mystery of the ships,
> 　And the magic of the sea.
> 　　And the voice of that wayward song
> 　　Is singing and saying still :
> 　　· A boy's will is the wind's will,
> And the thoughts of youth are long, long thoughts.' "

There were several clever lads in Portland at this
time who went to the same school, or schools, as
Henry Wadsworth Longfellow, and among them
was John Owen, who, I believe, was a cousin, and

who was his constant companion in after-life. He was about a year the elder, and he has outlived his illustrious friend less than a month, for while I am writing these paragraphs the journals contain the intelligence of his death on the 22d of April, at Cambridge. Another of his schoolfellows was probably Nathaniel Parker Willis, who was also a year his senior, and who was to achieve poetic distinction at about the same time as himself. Other Portland boys and men of this or a later period were Isaac M'Lellan, John Neal, and Seba Smith, all of whom figure in our poetic anthologies—self-appointed, patriotic laureates of the woods, waters, and warfare of their native land. They might have said of themselves, as Dr. Johnson said of himself and his fellow-students at Pembroke, "We were a nest of nightingales." Master Longfellow is known to have written verses in his childhood, and on his seventy-fifth birthday there was exhibited at Portland, I think in a room of the Maine Historical Society, a copy of one of these *juvenilia*, which I remember to have read at the time, and which I hope to recover before this Medley is finished. Like Dr. Bryant, Mr. Longfellow was proud of the genius of his son.

That young Mr. Longfellow had already obtained a good education, either at the public schools, or by diligent coaching under accomplished masters, is certain, or he could not have entered Bowdoin College, as he did, in his fourteenth year. Had his father followed his inclinations he would, no doubt, have sent him to his own *Alma Mater ;* but Cambridge is a long way from Portland, and Brunswick was nigh at hand,—so to Brunswick the lad was sent. It is a charming spot, I hear, on the right bank of the Androscoggin, at the head of tide-water, with shady woods in which there are winding walks, with falls that recall, on a small scale, the cataract of Velino, and with a bridge or two over the roaring and tumbling river, down which in spray drifted the clamped logs of the lumbermen. Bowdoin College was opened about the time when Mr. Longfellow went to Portland, and Seba Smith was graduated there three years before Henry Wadsworth was entered. It was a famous class in which he found himself, for before many years were over the names of four of its members had flown to the ends of the earth. These were Nathaniel Hawthorne, orphan son of a sea-captain of Salem, Mass ; John S. C. Abbott, son of pious parents, notorious twenty-five or thirty years ago for his " Life of Napoleon "; George B. Cheever, who turned the flood of public indignation upon Deacon Giles's Distillery, and was afterwards a pilgrim under

the shadow of Mont Blanc ; and Jonathan Cilley,
whose forte was political debate, and who went down
in the prime of his manhood before the deadly rifle
of Graves, of Kentucky. While Master Longfellow
was dreaming in Dering Woods, and learning many
tongues at Brunswick, a fellow-poet, who was about
twelve years his elder, was wandering in the groves
of Berkshire, and, later, was studying the law at
Great Barrington and Plymouth. The blood of John
Alden ran in the veins of both. Mr. William Cullen
Bryant is the greatest poet, it seems to me, that has
yet appeared in the New World. If there be a greater it is the man who now lies in his coffin at Concord,
whose genius was equal to that of Mr. Bryant, but
whose art never to the last put on the *toga virilis.*
Henry Wadsworth studied books ; William Cullen
studied Nature. There was not a flower in his father's garden, not a blade of grass in his fields, not
a water-course in his neighborhood, that did not
sparkle, and wave, and bloom in his imagination. He
immortalized the yellow violet, as it peeped up mod-
estly from the beechen buds ; he contained the twilight flight of the water-fowl ; he interpreted the
mysterious secret of the forests, and hills, and heavens—the universality of Death. No young man
ever chanted so grand an anthem as " Thanatopsis,"
which carried his fame about the earth while the

down of manhood was light upon his cheek. And in the summer of the year in which Henry Wadsworth went to Bowdoin he delivered before the young gentlemen who composed the society of the Phi Beta Kappa at Harvard the stateliest poem that was ever delivered. It will reach its address—"The Ages."

The modern poet labors under a disadvantage which did not attach to his predecessors. He cannot saunter up and down the world chanting his prepared impromptus, as the troubadors and minnesingers did, stopping at one court after another, and entrancing kings and queens, lords and ladies, knights, squires, pages, with strains of minstrelsy wedded to the music of lyre and lute. He cannot wander up and down the highways and byeways, through crowded city streets and solitary country roads, singing aloud, like the larks above him, romances of old-time chivalry, ballads of battles lost and won, traditions of faithless swains and faithful maids, pathetic, homely tragedies of breaking hearts, and death. No; his path has been crossed by the shadows of Faust, Caxton, Wynkin de Worde—professors of the Black Art. He must have a printer!

Without entering upon American Literature, which is too large to be traversed by a Medley like this, and without attempting the Life of Bryant, which Mr. Parke Godwin has nearly finished, I believe, the

reader of what immediately follows will be good
enough to conceive the condition of our letters half a
century ago, and imagine himself at Brunswick and
in Berkshire. There is no occasion for him to imagine or conceive the *United States Literary Gazette,* for copies of that periodical are doubtless to
be found in most public libraries. It was projected
and published by Mr. Theophilus Parsons, of Boston
—a graduate of Harvard, a lawyer, afterwards a theological writer, and a judge. If he be still living—and
I have no recollection of his decease—Judge Parsons
has almost completed his eighty-fifth year. The
United States Literary Gazette, a quarto sheet about
the size of the London *Athenæum,* was published
every two weeks. If my memory of it is to be depended upon, it began appropriately on April **1,**
1824. At any rate, Mr. Bryant's first contribution to
it was printed in the number which bears that date.
It was the Hebrew study, "Rizpah," and it was succeeded by other studies in rapid succession—so rapid,
indeed, that in eleven months they reached the number of twenty-one different poems, in various measures, amounting to over one thousand lines. This
would not have been many for a poet like Mr. Bryant
to produce in that time, if literature had been his
profession. But it was not. He was a lawyer in
good practice in his native county ; he was also a new-

ly married man. Mr. Longfellow's contributions to
the *Literary Gazette* began on November 15, 1824, and
ended on November 15, 1825. There were sixteen of
them, and they covered the space of a twelvemonth.
It would not be fair to compare the poems of the two
poets, remembering the difference between their
ages, but it is curious to contrast them; for the contrast brings out as nothing else could do the marked
characteristics of each, and the intellectual superiority of Mr. Bryant, who was always imaginative, while
Mr. Longfellow never was so until time had brushed
away the efflorescence of his fancy, and matured his
indolent, easy-going judgment. Mr. Bryant strode
along like the giant he was, leaving "Rizpah" to attend "The Old Man's Funeral" on April 15, and
passing from that solemnity to pursue "The Rivulet" on May 15. He turned his back upon "March"
on June 1, and related "An Indian Story" on
July 1. Then he floated away to "Summer
Wind" on July 15, and was "An Indian at the
Burial-place of his Fathers" on August 1. He
sang the "Hymn of the Waldenses" on September
1, and meditated upon "Monument Mountain" on
September 15. He found himself "After a Tempest" on October 1, and was dreaming in "Autumn Woods" on October 15. The "Song of the
Greek Amazon" fired his heart on December 1; he

tracked "The Murdered Traveller" on January 1
(1825); became the chapel-master of the heavens in
his "Hymn to the North Star" on January 15;
pursued and reached "The Lapse of Time" on February 15; and broke into jubilance on the 1st of
March with his "Song of the Stars." As I shall reprint in their proper place all the early poems of Mr.
Longfellow, with the exception of those which he
preserved in "Voices of the Night," fourteen years
later, I will only say here that when Mr. Bryant,
on November 15, was musing on "Mutation" and
"November," he was deep in "Thanksgiving"; that
when Mr. Bryant was penning his beautiful address "To a Cloud" he was painting "Italian
Scenery"; that when Mr. Bryant discovered "The
Murdered Traveller" he was caring for "The Lu-
natic Girl"; and that when Mr. Bryant was chanting his magnificent "Hymn to the North Star" he
was carolling about "The Venetian Gondolier."
The contrast between Master and Scholar was striking and instructive.

Mr. Richard Herne Shepherd, the bibliographer of
Tennyson, Ruskin, and Carlyle, collected from the
columns of the *Literary Gazette* the early poems of
Mr. Longfellow, and reprinted them in 1877 through
the time-honored house of Pickering. He was under
the impression that they had not been collected be-

fore, but he was mistaken. They were included in a volume of "Miscellaneous Poems," selected from the *Literary Gazette*, and published in Boston in 1826. Here are the firstlings of Mr. Longfellow in their original order and chronology :

THANKSGIVING.

WHEN first in ancient time, from Jubal's tongue
The tuneful anthem fill'd the morning air,
To sacred hymnings and elysian song
His music-breathing shell the minstrel woke,
Devotion breath'd aloud from every chord :
The voice of praise was heard in every tone,
And prayer, and thanks to Him the eternal one—
To Him that with bright inspiration touch'd
The high and gifted lyre of heavenly song,
And warm'd the soul with new vitality.
A stirring energy through Nature breath'd :
The voice of adoration from her broke,
Swelling aloud in every breeze, and heard
Long in the sullen waterfall—what time
Soft Spring or hoary Autumn threw on earth
Its bloom or blighting—when the Summer smil'd,
Or Winter o'er the year's sepulchre mourned.
The Deity was there!—a nameless spirit
Mov'd in the breasts of men to do Him homage;
And when the morning smil'd, or evening pale
Hung weeping o'er the melancholy urn,
They came beneath the broad, o'erarching trees,
And in their tremulous shadow worshipp'd oft

Where pale the vine clung round their simple altars,
And gray moss mantling hung.   Above was heard
The melody of winds, breath'd out as the green trees
Bow'd to their quivering touch in living beauty,　,
And birds sang forth their cheerful hymns.   Below
The bright and widely wandering rivulet
Struggl'd and gush'd amongst the tangled roots
That chok'd its reedy fountain, and dark rocks
Worn smooth by the constant current.   Even there
The listless wave, that stole with mellow voice
Where reeds grew rank on the rushy-fring'd brink,
And the green sedge bent to the wandering wind,
Sang with a cheerful song of sweet tranquillity.
Men felt the heavenly influence, and it stole
Like balm into their hearts till all was peace;
And even the air they breath'd—the light they saw—
Became religion, for the ethereal spirit
That to soft music wakes the chords of feeling,
And mellows everything to beauty, mov'd
With cheering energy within their breasts,　·
And made all holy there—for all was love.
The morning stars, that sweetly sang together;
The moon, that hung at night in the mid-sky;
Dayspring, and eventide, and all the fair
And beautiful forms of Nature, had a voice
Of eloquent worship.   Ocean with its tides
Swelling and deep, where low the infant storm
Hung on his dun, dark cloud, and heavily beat
The pulses of the sea, sent forth a voice
Of awful adoration to the Spirit
That, wrapt in darkness, mov'd upon its face.

And when the bow of evening arched the east,
Or, in the moonlight pale, the curling wave
Kiss'd with a sweet embrace the sea-worn beach,
And soft the song of winds came o'er the waters,
The mingled melody of wind and wave
Touch'd like a heavenly anthem on the ear;
For it arose a tuneful hymn of worship.
And have *our* hearts grown cold ? Are there on earth
No pure reflections caught from heavenly light ?
Have our mute lips no hymn, our souls no song ?
Let him that in the summer day of youth
Keeps pure the holy fount of youthful feeling,
And him that in the nightfall of his years
Lies down in his last sleep, and shuts in peace
His dim, pale eyes on life's short wayfaring,
Praise Him that rules the destiny of man.

SUNDAY EVENING, OCTOBER, 1824.

AUTUMNAL NIGHTFALL.

ROUND Autumn's mouldering urn
Loud mourns the chill and cheerless gale,
When nightfall shades the quiet vale,
    And stars in beauty burn.

'Tis the year's eventide.
The wind, like one that sighs in pain
O'er joys that ne'er will bloom again,
    Mourns on the far hillside.

And yet my pensive eye
Rests on the faint blue mountain long,
And for the fairy-land of song,
        That lies beyond, I sigh.

The moon unveils her brow;
In the mid-sky her urn glows bright,
And in her sad and mellowing light
        The valley sleeps below.

Upon the hazel gray
The lyre of Autumn hangs unstrung,
And o'er its tremulous chords are flung
        The fringes of decay.

I stand deep musing here,
Beneath the dark and motionless beech,
Whilst wandering winds of nightfall reach
        My melancholy ear.

The air breathes chill and free;
A Spirit in soft music calls
From Autumn's gray and moss-grown halls,
        And round her wither'd tree.

The hoar and mantled oak,
With moss and twisted ivy brown,
Bends in its lifeless beauty down
        Where weeds the fountain choke.

That fountain's hollow voice
Echoes the sound of precious things—
Of early feeling's tuneful springs
        Chok'd with our blighted joys.

Leaves, that the night-wind bears
To earth's cold bosom with a sigh,
Are types of our mortality,
    And of our fading years.

The tree that shades the plain,
Wasting and hoar as time decays,
Spring shall renew with cheerful days—
    But not my joys again.

DECEMBER 1.

ITALIAN SCENERY.

NIGHT rests in beauty on Mont Alto.
Beneath its shade the beauteous Arno sleeps
In Vallombrosa's bosom, and dark trees
Bend with a calm and quiet shadow down
Upon the beauty of that silent river.
Still in the west a melancholy smile
Mantles the lips of day, and twilight pale
Moves like a spectre in the dusky sky ;
While eve's sweet star on the fast-fading year
Smiles calmly. Music steals at intervals
Across the water, with a tremulous swell,
From out the upland dingle of tall firs,
And a faint footfall sounds where dim and dark
Hangs the gray willow from the river's brink,
O'ershadowing its current. Slowly there
The lover's gondola drops down the stream,
Silent, save when its dipping oar is heard
Or in its eddy sighs the rippling wave.

Mouldering and moss-grown, through the lapse of years,
In motionless beauty stands the giant oak,
Whilst those that saw its green and flourishing youth
Are gone and are forgotten.   Soft the fount,
Whose secret springs the starlight pale discloses,
Gushes in hollow music, and beyond
The broader river sweeps its silent way,
Mingling a silver current with that sea
Whose waters have no tides, coming nor going.
On noiseless wing along that fair blue sea
The halcyon flits ; and where the wearied storm
Left a loud moaning, all is peace again.

A calm is on the deep !   The winds that came
O'er the dark sea-surge with a tremulous breathing,
And mourn'd on the dark cliff where weeds grew rank,
And to the autumnal death-dirge the deep sea
Heaved its long billows—with a cheerless song
Have pass'd away to the cold earth again,
Like a wayfaring mourner.   Silently
Up from the calm sea's dim and distant verge,
Full and unveil'd, the moon's broad disk emerges.
On Tivoli, and where the fairy hues
Of Autumn glow upon Abruzzi's woods,
The silver light is spreading.   Far above,
Encompass'd with their thin, cold atmosphere,
The Apennines uplift their snowy brows,
Glowing with colder beauty, where unheard
The eagle screams in the fathomless ether,
And stays his wearied wing.   Here let us pause !
The spirit of these solitudes—the soul

That dwells within these steep and difficult places—
Speaks a mysterious language to mine own,
And brings unutterable musings. Earth
Sleeps in the shades of nightfall, and the sea
Spreads like a thin blue haze beneath my feet,
Whilst the gray columns and the mouldering tombs
Of the Imperial City, hidden deep
Beneath the mantle of their shadows, rest.
My spirit looks on earth ! A heavenly voice
Comes silently : " Dreamer, is earth thy dwelling ?
Lo ! nurs'd within that fair and fruitful bosom
Which has sustain'd thy being, and within
The colder breast of Ocean, lie the germs
Of thine own dissolution ! E'en the air,
That fans the clear blue sky and gives thee strength—
Up from the sullen lake of mouldering reeds,
And the wide waste of forest, where the osier
Thrives in the damp and motionless atmosphere—
Shall bring the dire and wasting pestilence
And blight thy cheek.   Dream thou of higher things ;
This world is not thy home!" And yet my eye
Rests upon earth again ! How beautiful,
Where wild Velino heaves its sullen waves
Down the high cliff of gray and shapeless granite,
Hung on the curling mist, the moonlight bow
Arches the perilous river! A soft light
Silvers the Albanian mountains, and the haze
That rests upon their summits mellows down
The austerer features of their beauty.   Faint
And dim-discover'd glow the Sabine Hills,
And, listening to the sea's monotonous shell,

High on the cliffs of Terracina stands
The castle of the Royal Goth * in ruins.

But night is in her wane ; day's early flush
Glows like a hectic on her fading cheek,
Wasting its beauty.   And the opening dawn
With cheerful lustre lights the royal city,
Where with its proud tiara of dark towers
It sleeps upon its own romantic bay.

DECEMBER 15.

THE LUNATIC GIRL.

MOST beautiful, most gentle!   Yet how lost
To all that gladdens the fair earth; the eye
That watch'd her being; the maternal care
That kept and nourish'd her; and the calm light
That steals from our own thoughts, and softly rests
On youth's green valleys and smooth-sliding waters.
Alas! few suns of life, and fewer winds,
Had wither'd or had wasted the fresh rose
That bloom'd upon her cheek ; but one chill frost
Came in that early autumn, when ripe thought
Is rich and beautiful, and blighted it;
And the fair stock grew languid day by day,
And droop'd, and droop'd, and shed its many leaves.
'Tis said that some have died of love, and some,
That once from beauty's high romance had caught
Love's passionate feelings and heart-wasting cares,

* Theodoric.

Have spurn'd life's threshold with a desperate foot;
And others have gone mad—and she was one!
Her lover died at sea! and they had felt
A coldness for each other when they parted;
But love return'd again, and to her ear
Came tidings that the ship which bore her lover
Had suddenly gone down at sea, and all were lost.
I saw her in her native vale, when high
The aspiring lark up from the reedy river
Mounted on cheerful pinion; and she sat
Casting smooth pebbles into a clear fountain,
And marking how they sunk; and oft she sigh'd
For him that perish'd thus in the vast deep.
She had a sea-shell that her lover brought
From the far-distant ocean, and she press'd
Its smooth, cold lips unto her ear, and thought
It whisper'd tidings of the dark blue sea;
And, sad, she cried: "The tides are out! and now
I see his corse upon the stormy beach!"
Around her neck a string of rose-lipp'd shells,
And coral, and white pearl was loosely hung,
And close beside her lay a delicate fan,
Made of the halcyon's blue wing; and when
She look'd upon it, it would calm her thoughts
As that bird calms the ocean—for it gave
Mournful yet pleasant memory.   Once I mark'd,
When through the mountain hollows and green woods,
That bent beneath its footsteps, the loud wind
Came with a voice as of the restless deep,
She raised her head, and on her pale, cold cheek
A beauty of diviner seeming came:

And then she spread her hands, and smil'd, as if
She welcom'd a long-absent friend—and then
Shrunk timorously back again, and wept.
I turn'd away: a multitude of thoughts,
Mournful and dark, were crowding on my mind,
And as I left that lost and ruin'd one—
A living monument that still on earth
There is warm love and deep sincerity—
She gazed upon the west, where the blue sky
Held, like an ocean, in its wide embrace
Those fairy islands of bright cloud, that lay
So calm and quietly in the thin ether.
And then she pointed where, alone and high,
One little cloud sail'd onward, like a lost
And wandering bark, and fainter grew, and fainter,
And soon was swallow'd up in the blue depths.
And when it sunk away she turn'd again
With sad despondency and tears to earth.

Three long and weary months—yet not a whisper
Of stern reproach for that cold parting! Then
She sat no longer by her favorite fountain!
She was at rest for ever.

January 1, 1825.

THE VENETIAN GONDOLIER.

Here rest the weary oar!—soft airs
'Breathe out in the o'erarching sky;
And Night!—sweet Night—serenely wears
A smile of peace; her noon is nigh.

Where the tall fir in quiet stands,
  And waves, embracing the chaste shores,
Move o'er sea-shells and bright sands,
  Is heard the sound of dipping oars.

Swift o'er the wave the light bark springs;
  Love's midnight hour draws lingering near:
And list! his tuneful viol strings
  The young Venetian Gondolier.

Lo! on the silver-mirror'd deep,
  On earth and her embosom'd lakes,
And where the silent rivers sweep,
  From the thin cloud fair moonlight breaks.

Soft music breathes around, and dies
  On the calm bosom of the sea;
Whilst in her cell the novice sighs
  Her vespers to her rosary.

At their dim altars bow fair forms,
  In tender charity for those
That, helpless left to life's rude storms,
  Have never found this calm repose.

The bell swings to its midnight chime,
  Reliev'd against the deep blue sky!
Haste! dip the oar again! 'tis time
  To seek Genevra's balcony.

JANUARY 15.

DIRGE OVER A NAMELESS GRAVE.

By yon still river, where the wave
  Is winding slow at evening's close,
The beech, upon a nameless grave,
  Its sadly-moving shadow throws.

O'er the fair woods the sun looks down
  Upon the many-twinkling leaves,
And twilight's mellow shades are brown,
  Where darkly the green turf upheaves.

The river glides in silence there,
  And hardly waves the sapling tree;
Sweet flowers are springing, and the air
  Is full of balm — but where is she!

They bade her wed a son of pride,
  And leave the hopes she cherish'd long:
She loved but one, and would not hide
  A love which knew no wrong.

And months went sadly on—and years:
  And she was wasting day by day
At length she died, and many tears
  Were shed that she should pass away.

Then came a gray old man, and knelt
  With bitter weeping by her tomb:
And others mourn'd for him, who felt
  That he had seal'd a daughter's doom.

The funeral train has long passed on,
    And time wiped dry the father's tear!
Farewell, lost maiden!   There is one
    That mourns thee yet—and he is here.

MARCH 15.

A SONG OF SAVOY.

As the dim twilight shrouds
    The mountain's purple crest,
And Summer's white and folded clouds
    Are glowing in the west,
Loud shouts come up the rocky dell,
And voices hail the evening-bell.

Faint is the goatherd's song,
    And sighing comes the breeze:
The silent river sweeps along
    Amid its bending trees—
And the full moon shines faintly there,
And music fills the evening air.

Beneath the waving firs
    The tinkling cymbals sound;
And as the wind the foliage stirs,
    I feel the dancers bound
Where the green branches arch'd above
Bend over this fair scene of love.

And he is there that sought
My young heart long ago !
But he has left me, though I thought
He ne'er could leave me so.
Ah! lovers' vows—how frail are they!
And his—were made but yesterday.

Why comes he not ? I call
In tears upon him yet;
'Twere better ne'er to love at all
Than love and then forget!
Why comes he not ? Alas! I should
Reclaim him still, if weeping could.

But see! he leaves the glade
And beckons me away:
He comes to seek his mountain maid!
I cannot chide his stay.
Glad sounds along the valley swell,
And voices hail the evening-bell.

MARCH 15.

THE INDIAN HUNTER.

WHEN the Summer harvest was gather'd in,
And the sheaf of the gleaner grew white and thin,
And the ploughshare was in its furrow left
Where the stubble land had been lately cleft,
An Indian hunter, with unstrung bow,
Look'd down where the valley lay stretch'd below.

He was a stranger there, and all that day
Had been out on the hills, a perilous way;
But the foot of the deer was far and fleet,
And the wolf kept aloof from the hunter's feet,
And bitter feelings pass'd o'er him then
As he stood by the populous haunts of men.

The winds of Autumn came over the woods
As the sun stole out from their solitudes,
The moss was white on the maple's trunk,
And dead from its arms the pale vine shrunk,
And ripen'd the mellow fruit hung, and red
Were the tree's wither'd leaves round it shed.

The foot of the reaper moved slow on the lawn,
And the sickle cut down the yellow corn;
The mower sung loud by the meadow-side,
Where the mists of evening were spreading wide,
And the voice of the herdsman came up the lea,
And the dance went round by the greenwood tree.

Then the hunter turn'd away from that scene,
Where the home of his fathers once had been,
And heard, by the distant and measur'd stroke,
That the woodman hew'd down the giant oak,
And burning thoughts flash'd over his mind
Of the white man's faith, and love unkind.

The moon of the harvest grew high and bright,
As her golden horn pierc'd the cloud of white;
A footstep was heard in the rustling brake,

Where the beech overshadow'd the misty lake,
And a mourning voice, and a plunge from shore;
And the hunter was seen on the hills no more.

When years had pass'd on, by that still lakeside
The fisher look'd down through the silver tide,
And there, on the smooth yellow sand display'd,
A skeleton, wasted and white, was laid;
And 'twas seen, as the waters moved deep and slow,
That the hand was still grasping a hunter's bow.

May 15.

JECKOYVA.

The Indian chief Jeckoyva, as tradition says, perished alone on the mountain which now bears his name. Night overtook him whilst hunting among the cliffs, and he was not heard of till after a long time, when his half-decayed corpse was found at the foot of a high rock, over which he must have fallen. Mount Jeckoyva is near the White Hills.

They made the warrior's grave beside
The dashing of his native tide:
And there was mourning in the glen—
The strong wail of a thousand men—
   O'er him thus fallen in his pride,
Ere mist of age, or blight, or blast
Had o'er his mighty spirit pass'd.

They made the warrior's grave beneath
The bending of the wild elm's wreath,
When the dark hunter's piercing eye

Had found that mountain rest on high,
    Where, scattered by the sharp wind's breath,
Beneath the rugged cliff were thrown
The strong belt and the mouldering bone.

Where was the warrior's foot when first
The red sun on the mountain burst?
Where, when the sultry noontime came
On the green vales with scorching flame,
    And made the woodlands faint with thirst?
'Twas where the wind is keen and loud,
And the gray eagle breasts the cloud.

Where was the warrior's foot when night
Veil'd in thick cloud the mountain-height?
None heard the loud and sudden crash,
None saw the fallen warrior dash
    Down the bare rock so high and white!
But he that droop'd not in the chase
Made on the hills his burial-place.

They found him there, when the long day
Of cold desertion pass'd away,
And traces on that barren cleft
Of struggling hard with death were left—
    Deep marks and footprints in the clay!
And they have laid this feathery helm
By the dark river and green elm.

AUGUST J.

THE SEA-DIVER.

My way is on the bright blue sea,
  My sleep upon its rocking tide;
And many an eye has follow'd me
  Where billows clasp the worn seaside.

My plumage bears the crimson blush
  When ocean by the sea is kiss'd!
When fades the evening's purple flush,
  My dark wing cleaves the silver mist.

Full many a fathom down beneath
  The bright arch of the splendid deep
My ear has heard the sea-shell breathe
  O'er living myriads in their sleep.

They rested by the coral throne
  And by the pearly diadem,
Where the pale sea-grape had o'ergrown
  The glorious dwellings made for them.

At night upon my storm-drench'd wing
  I pois'd above a helmless bark,
And soon I saw the shatter'd thing
  Had pass'd away and left no mark.

And when the wind and storm were done,
  A ship, that had rode out the gale,
Sunk down, without a signal-gun,
  And none was left to tell the tale.

I saw the pomp of day depart,
  The cloud resign its golden crown,
When to the ocean's beating heart
  The sailor's wasted course went down.

Peace be to those whose graves are made
  Beneath the bright and silver sea!
Peace, that their relics there were laid
  With no vain pride and pageantry.

AUGUST 15.

MUSINGS.

I SAT by my window one night,
  And watch'd how the stars grew high;
And the earth and skies were a splendid sight
  To a sober and musing eye.

From heaven the silver moon shone down
  With gentle and mellow ray,
And beneath the crowded roofs of the town
  In broad light and shadow lay.

A glory was on the silent sea,
  And mainland and island too,
Till a haze came over the lowland lea
  And shrouded that beautiful blue.

Bright in the moon the Autumn wood
  Its crimson scarf unroll'd,
And the trees like a splendid army stood
  In a panoply of gold!

I saw them waving their banners high,
  As their crests to the night wind bow'd,
And a distant sound on the air went by,
  Like the whispering of a crowd.

Then I watch'd from my window how fast
  The lights all around me fled,
As the wearied man to his slumber pass'd,
  And the sick one to his bed.

All faded save one, that burn'd
  With distant and steady light;
But that, too, went out—and I turn'd
  Where my own lamp within shone bright!

Thus, thought I, our joys must die;
  Yes, the brightest from earth we win:
Till each turns away, with a sigh,
  To the lamp that burns brightly within.

NOVEMBER 15

SONG.

WHERE, from the eye of day,
  The dark and silent river
Pursues through tangled woods a way
  O'er which the tall trees quiver;

The silver mist, that breaks
  From out that woodland cover,
Betrays the hidden path it takes,
  And hangs the current over!

> So oft the thoughts that burst
> From hidden springs of feeling,
> Like silent streams, unseen at first,
> From our cold hearts are stealing;
>
> But soon the clouds that veil
> The eye of Love, when glowing,
> Betray the long-unwhispered tale
> Of thoughts in darkness flowing!

ApRIL 1, 1826.

The poems excluded from those that we have printed, and from the list that we have given, but included in "Voices of the Night," are "Woods in Winter" (February 1, 1825), "An April Day" (April 15), "Hymn of the Moravian Nuns" (June 1), "Sunrise on the Hills" (July 1), and "Autumn" (October 1). The poetry of the *Literary Gazette* (Mr. Godwin informs me) attracted so much attention that when the collection of which I have spoken appeared the *North American Review* thought the publication of it a signal event in the history of our letters. Mr. Bryant was of the same opinion, for in noticing it afterwards in the New York *Review*, of which he was editor, he remarked: "We do not know, of all the numerous English periodical works, any one that has furnished within the same time as much really beautiful poetry. We might cite in proof of this the 'April Day,' the 'Hymn of the

Moravian Nuns," and the 'Sunrise on the Hills,' by H. W. L. (we know not who he is), or more par- ticularly those exquisite *morceaux*, 'True Greatness,' 'The Soul of Song,' 'The Graves of the Patriots,' and 'The Desolate City,' by P., whom it would be affectation not to recognize as Dr. Percival.'' I have read the four poems by Dr. Percival, and I see little or nothing in them, except a determination to surpass Campbell in brevity, and soar away from him on the pinions of inflated rhetoric. Such a query as this concerning the Soul of Song is certainly not to be hastily answered :

> "Loves it the gay saloon,
> Where wine and dances steal away the night,
> And bright as summer noon
> Burns round the pictured walls a blaze of light ?"

Dr. Percival was nearly twelve years older than Mr. Longfellow ; he was a century younger in practical knowledge of poetry—one of those scholarly men of genius who disappoint everybody, themselves most of all. The estimation in which Mr. Longfellow's early verse was held was well stated by his college friend, Mr. Cheever, who, five years later than the publica- tion of the volume specified above, compiled a mis- cellaneous medley of melodies of home manufacture, which he unthinkingly entitled "The Commonplace

Book of American Poetry," and which Mr. Poe un-
feelingly declared had at least the merit of not belying
its title, for it *was* exceedingly commonplace. Mr.
Cheever included seven of Mr. Longfellow's poems
therein, and subjoined to the last the following note :
" Most of Mr. Longfellow's poetry—indeed, we believe nearly all that has been published—appeared
during his college life in the *United States Literary
Gazette.* It displays a very refined taste, and a very
pure vein of poetical feeling. It possesses what has
been a rare quality in the American poets—simplicity of expression, without any attempt to startle
the reader, or to produce an effect by far-sought epithets. There is much sweetness in his imagery and
language ; and sometimes he is hardly excelled by
any one for the quiet accuracy exhibited in his pictures of natural objects. His poetry will not easily
be forgotten ; some of it will be remembered with
that of Dana and Bryant."

The year in which Mr. Cheever published his Commonplace Book was an eventful year for American
Song. Mr. William Cullen Bryant published his
second collection of Poems, and Mr. Edgar Allan Poe
published his second (or third) collection of Poems,
both in New York, in the same year, and through
the same publisher, Elam Bliss. Mr. Bryant was the
editor of the *Evening Post ;* Mr. Poe was the editor

of nothing. He had just been expelled from West Point by court-martial, charged with gross neglect of all duties, and disobedience of orders, and was tinkering over his old verses (perhaps in New York), and receiving subscriptions of two dollars and fifty cents for his projected *opuscule* from his whilom fellow-cadets. What *he* thought of the *Cheever-Literary Gazette* Poets may easily be divined. "I never heard him speak in terms of praise of any English writer, living or dead," was the bitter testimony of one who knew him at this time. Every other man was a plagiarist; *he* was original.

The eminence of Mr. Bryant was seen in the influence that he exercised over his contemporaries, and over his intellectual son, Mr. Longfellow. Mr. Bryant's well-head of inspiration was Nature; the earliest fountains from which he drank were the Latin and Greek classics; after these Pope, Dryden, Gray, Collins, Cowper, Wordsworth. The spirit that sparkled in their lucid waters quenched and increased his thirst. His first American masters were Timothy Dwight and Philip Freneau—Dwight in "Greenfield Hill," particularly in the third part of that rustic epic, which is devoted to the destruction of the Pequods, and Freneau in such poems as "The Dying Indian," and "The Indian Burying-Ground." Mr. Bryant's first scholars in nature-worship and in aboriginal lore were Miss Lydia Huntley, Mr. John Gardiner Calkins Brainard, Mr. Carlos Wilcox, and Mr. Henry Wadsworth Longfellow. There was a clever monitor and a sprightly monitress in the school to which Mr. Longfellow went, and from them he derived much of his second-hand knowledge. One was his old school-fellow, Nathaniel Parker Willis ; the other was a young English gentlewoman, of Irish and Italian descent, who was penning Welsh melodies at Bronwylfa, Miss Felicea Dorothea Browne. Her sensitive genius is felt in "An April Day" as surely as the influence of Willis, heightened by the strength of Bryant, is felt in "Autumn" and "The Spirit of Poetry." It is impossible not to recognize Willis in lines like these :

> " It fills the nice and delicate ear of thought,
>   When the fast-ushering star of morning comes
>   O'er-riding the gray hills with golden scarf."

There is mere millinery. Bryant overshadows everything. His "March" is repeated in "Woods in Winter." The testimony of any stanza of the last is convincing. Take the first :

> " When winter winds are piercing chill,
>   And through the hawthorn blows the gale,
>   With solemn feet I tread the hill
>   That overbrows the lonely vale."

And what but the close of "Thanatopsis" can have
suggested the close of "Autumn"?

> " For him the wind, ay, and the yellow leaves,
>   Shall have a voice and give him eloquent teachings.
>   He shall so hear the solemn hymn that Death
>   Has lifted up for all that he shall go
>   To his long resting-place without a tear."

He went to his long resting-place nearly fifty-seven
years later, with the tears of the world.

I have not written these last paragraphs with the
intention of depreciating Mr. Longfellow, or casting
the shadow of a doubt upon his originality, but
simply to point out that all poets, small and great
alike, start by echoing the songs of others. Homer's masters, if we could discover them, were old
rhapsodists. We know the lords paramount of the
Greek and Roman tragic writers, idyllic pipers, bit-
ing satirists. Chaucer was the child of Petrarcha and
Boccaccio, Gower of Chaucer, Surrey of the Italian
sonneteers, Shakespeare of Daniel and Marlowe, Milton of Du Bartas, Cowley of Spenser, Pope of Dryden, Cowper of Thomson, Burns of Ramsay, Ferguson, and early balladists, Wordsworth of all poets,
Keats of Chaucer and Spenser, Tennyson of Keats,
and Longfellow of Bryant. It is an illustrious
pedigree.

Graduating with honors in his eighteenth year, to the delight of his college friends, Mr. Longfellow betook himself to Portland, and entered the office of his father to study the law. But it was not to be, for the faculty of Bowdoin thought so highly of their poetic scholar that they appointed him Professor of Modern Languages and Literature, with the privilege of going abroad for three years that he might qualify himself for his duties. He accepted—he would have been mad not to have accepted, for he was averse from the law, and not disposed to become a teacher either of wealthy or beautiful pupils; so in the following year he set sail for Europe. Americans of fifty years ago were not so accustomed to travel as their descendants have grown to be. Now and then one did cross the Atlantic billows, and one of the first to go from Portland was Mr. John Neal, who had wandered to London while Mr. Longfellow was at college, and was supporting himself by his pen in *Blackwood's Magazine* and other British periodicals. Him, no doubt, Mr. Longfellow met, either at his chambers, or the libraries, or in the crowded study of Mr. Jeremy Bentham. Mr. Irving he certainly met in 1827. "I had parted with him at Paris early in the year," writes Mr. Pierre Irving. "His sojourn in Madrid had commenced with the 6th of March, Mr. Irving, in a letter to me of the 8th, having this mention of him:

'Mr. Longfellow arrived safe and cheerily the day before yesterday, having met with no robbers.' "   Mr.
Pierre Irving then proceeds to pay Mr. Longfellow a
compliment for his beautiful allusion to his distinguished uncle, and quotes a passage from a discourse
delivered by him before the Massachusetts Historical Society, and expressing his admiration for the
"Sketch-Book," published when he was a school-
boy.   "Many years afterwards I had the pleasure of
meeting Mr. Irving in Spain, and found the author,
whom I had loved, repeated in the man.   The same
playful humor, the same touch of sentiment, the
same poetic atmosphere, and, what I admired still
more, the entire absence of all literary jealousy, of
all that mean avarice of fame which counts what is
given to another as so much taken from one's self—

> " 'And, trembling, hears on every breeze
> The laurels of Miltiades.'

"At this time Mr. Irving was at Madrid, engaged
upon his 'Life of Columbus,' and if the work itself
did not bear ample testimony to his zealous and conscientious labor I could do so from personal observation.   He seemed to be always at work.   'Sit down,'
he would say ; 'I will talk with you in a moment, but
I must first finish this sentence.'

"One summer morning, passing his house at the

early hour of six, I saw his study already wide open. On my mentioning it to him afterwards he said : 'Yes, I am always at my work as early as six.' Since then I have often remembered that sunny morning and that open window, so suggestive of his sunny temperament and his open heart, and equally so of his patient and persistent toil, and have recalled those striking words of Dante :

> " 'Seggendo in piuma,
> In fama non si vien, ne sotto coltre;
> Senza la qual, chi sua vita consuma,
> Cotal vestigio in terra, di se lascia
> Qual fummo in aere el in acqua la schiuma.'

> " 'Seated upon down,
> Or in his bed, man cometh not to fame;
> Without which, whoso his life consumes,
> Such vestige of himself on earth shall leave
> As smoke in air and in the water foam.'"

A graceful tribute from a scholar to his dead master.

A reasonable amount of originality was expected of, and demanded from, an American tourist in the second quarter of the century. He was not asked to entertain but to instruct his readers. He might be anything that he could fish up from his inkstand— whimsical, desultory, pedantic, even a little dull, if he must needs be. What was looked for were his impressions, his notions about effete aristocracies, ideals of bygone time to which Ideality was a stranger. I shall not go here into the itinerary of the travelling poet further than to say that it was directed through England, France, Spain, Italy, Germany, and Holland. A ripe scholar and a good one, he returned to his duties at Brunswick in 1829. From this date begins his fifty-three years' devotion to literature as tutor, teacher, lecturer, critic, poet, translator, magazinist, and man of letters generally—honorable service in a high cause. I hope before I have done to trace the bibliography of his work with tolerable accuracy; at present I can only speak of the first of his works in my own possession. It is a shabby 12mo of 104 pages, bound in red cloth, and is entitled "Syllabus de la Grammaire Italienne. Par H. W. Longfellow, Professor de Langues Modernes à Bowdoin-College. A l'Usage de Ceux qui Possèdent la Langue Française. Boston: Gray et Bowen. MDCCCXXXII." It was ushered into the world by this Avertissement: "J'ai préparé cet Abrigé de la Grammaire Italienne, non pour instruire ceux qui auraient à parler cette langue, mais pour faciliter les progrès de ceux, qui voudront l'apprendre à lire. Pour atteindre ce but il suffit d'en avoir exposé succinctement les principes. Il serait superflu de les développer dans tous leur étendue.

"J'ai employé l'accent aigu sur presque tous les mots Italiens, pour marquer les syllabes sur lesquelles il faut appuyer la voix dans la prononciation ; mais il faut observer que les Italiens ne s'en servent que très rarement. On trouvera les règles pour l'usage de l'accent aigu dans la traité de l'Orthographie ; voyez chapitre viii., page 104. H. W. L."

Of the fate of this little pony, whereupon those who had mounted it might amble easily from France to Italy, I have no knowledge. I dare say it took *le grand prix*, for it was not handicapped, and was ridden by a jockey of light weight, behind whom, booted and spurred, was not yet riding Black Care. Neither were " Yoicks forward!" and " Ho, Tally-Ho!" among the greetings that saluted it. Gray et Bowen were not plungers.

Future bibliographers will, no doubt, work out the succession of Mr. Longfellow's writings, from his greatest work—when time shall have determined which that is—down to the smallest scrap that proceeded from his pen. My business now is chiefly with his books, and not with his papers in periodicals—such, for instance, as the *North American Review*, in which, I believe, the earliest of these papers was published. His next book after the "Syllabus de la Grammaire Italienne" was a model of scholarly and spirited translation. Its full title was: "Cop-

las de Don Jorge Manrique. Translated from the
Spanish. With an Introductory Essay on the Moral
and Devotional Poetry of Spain." The name of the
author follows, and the imprint of "Boston : Allan and Ticknor. 1833." Of the accuracy of Mr.
Longfellow's reproduction of the grave and stately
original I am no adequate judge ; but,. if I may
trust the impression which it has always made upon
me, it certainly reflects the moral and devotional
spirit of Don Jorge Manrique, and his deep though
temperate grief on the death of his father, Roderigo
Manrique, Conde de Parades and Maestre de Santi-
ago, who died in 1476, according to Mariana, in the
town of Uclés, but according to his son, who survived him three years, in Ocaña. Mr. George Ticknor, the historian of Spanish literature, directs our
attention to the simplicity and directness of its title,
" The Stanzas of Manrique," as if it needed no more
distinctive name. " Nor does it. Instead of being a
loud exhibition of his sorrows, or, what would have
been more in the spirit of the age, a conceited exhibition of his learning, it is a simple and natural
complaint of the mutability of all earthly happiness ;
the mere overflowing of a heart filled with despondency at being suddenly brought to feel the worthless-
ness of what it has most valued and pursued. His
father occupies hardly half the canvas of the poem,

and some of the stanzas devoted more directly to
him are the only portion of it we could wish away."
Mr. Ticknor quotes three stanzas of this solemn dirge
over mortality, and pronounces Mr. Longfellow's
translation a beautiful one. It is more than that—
it is noble and weighty in the lines on the court of
John II. :

> " Where is the King Don Juan ?   Where
>   Each royal prince and noble heir
>   Of Aragon ?
>   Where are the courtly gallantries ?
>   The deeds of love and high emprise
>   In battle done ?
>   Tourney and joust that charm'd the eye,
>   And scarf, and gorgeous panoply,
>   And nodding plume :
>   What were they but a pageant scene ?
>   What but the garlands gay and green
>   That deck the tomb ?

> " Where are the high-born dames, and where
>   Their gay attire, and jewell'd hair,
>   And odors sweet ?
>   Where are the gentle knights that came
>   To kneel and breathe love's ardent flame
>   Low at their feet ?
>   Where is the song of Troubadour ?
>   Where are the lute and gay tambour

> They loved of yore ?
> Where is the mazy dance of old,
> The flowing robes inwrought with gold
> The dancers wore ? ”

The little volume which ushered this thoughtful strain into the world contained besides seven translations of Spanish sonnets of no great poetical value. When Mr. Longfellow reprinted the collection he omitted two which have never reappeared among his writings. They are by Francisco de Medrano:

I.

ART AND NATURE.

> THE works of human artifice soon tire
> The curious eye ; the fountain's sparkling rill,
> And gardens, when adorn'd by human skill,
> Reproach the feeble hand, the vain desire.
>   But, O the free and wild magnificence
> Of Nature, in her lavish hours, doth steal,
> In admiration silent and intense,
> The soul of him, who hath a soul to feel.
>   The river moving on its ceaseless way,
> The verdant reach of meadows fair and green,
> And the blue hills that bound the sylvan scene—
>   These speak of grandeur that defies decay ;
> Proclaim the Eternal Architect on high,
> Who stamps on all his works his own eternity.

II.

THE TWO HARVESTS.

BUT yesterday these few and hoary sheaves
Waved in the golden harvest; from the plain
I saw the blade shoot upward, and the grain
Put forth the unripe ear and tender leaves.

Then the glad upland smil'd upon the view,
And to the air the broad green leaves unroll'd,
A peerless emerald in each silken fold,
And on each palm a pearl of morning dew.

And thus sprang up and ripened in brief space
All that beneath the reaper's sickle died,
All that smiled beauteous in the summertide.

And what are we ?—a copy of that race,
The later harvest of a longer year!
And, O how many fall before the ripened ear.

A half-hour's glance over the early volumes of the
Knickerbocker Magazine has put me upon the literary trail of Mr. Longfellow after the publication of
this volume of Spanish translations. I struck it in
the number for May, 1834, in the first of a series of
scattered paragraphs under the general heading of
"The Blank-Book of a Country Schoolmaster."
As the reader may like to see one of these paragraphs, I will copy the fifth :

" MIDNIGHT DEVOTION.

" If there be one hour more fitted to devotion than

the rest, it is this—the silent, solemn, solitary hour of midnight in midwinter. Not a light can be seen in the village—the world is asleep around me. How breathless and how still! Not air enough to shake down the feathery snow from the branches of the trees and the leafless vine at my window.

> " The moon, a Virgin Queen,
> Reigns absolute in her celestial city.
> One lonely star, beside the western gate,
> Stands sentinel. All else around the throne
> Submissive veil their faces, for in her
> Reflected shine the majesty and light
> Of her departed lord, the glorious sun.
> The air itself is awed into a whisper!
> And yet amid the stillness comes a sound,
> Like the sad music of a muffled drum,
> Distant and indistinct. It is the voice
> Of many waters down the shelving rock
> Falling, still falling through the silent night,
> Fit music for the solemn march of Time.
>
> Father, who art in heaven! with contrite heart
> I bow before thee! Hallowed be thy name;
> I have fled from thee—but thou hast not cursed me;
> I have forsaken thee—yet thou hast blessed me;
> Forgotten thee—yet thou hast loved me still!"

This little leaf from the schoolmaster's blank-book possesses no intellectual value, though it is not without interest as a midnight record of Professor Longfellow's life at Bowdoin, and it is very curious as containing the germ of a famous stanza in a future poem—a stanza which has hitherto been sup-

posed to be a mere echo of four lines in the deathless
" Exequy of Bishop King " :

> ' But hark! My Pulse like a soft Drum
> Beats my approch, tells *Thee* I come;
> And slow howere my marches be,
> I shall at last sit down by *Thee*."

> " Art is long, and Time is fleeting,
>   And our hearts, though stout and brave,
>   Still, like muffled drums, are beating
>   Funeral marches to the grave."

The publication in parts of "Salmagundi" in 1807,
of "The Sketch-Book" in 1819, and of "The Idle
Man" in 1821, suggested to Mr. Longfellow the publication of his observations of travel in 1834. I
find a notice of the second part of "Outre-Mer,"
which bore the double imprint of Boston and New
York, in the July number of the *Knickerbocker:*
" There is not in our country a writer who so nearly
approaches the ease and grace of style, the purity
of sentiment and language, which distinguish the
' Sketch-Book ' and ' Bracebridge. Hall ' as the author of 'Outre-Mer.' We remember to have seen
many years since a touching sketch from his pen,
which was copied from an English periodical into
which it had found its way, and circulated widely
in American journals as the production of Wash-

ington Irving. His humor is of the same oblique,
happy cast, and his pathos has the power to awaken
the same thrilling echoes in the human bosom.'' The
kindly writer of this enthusiastic notice was probably Mr. Willis Gaylord Clark, who was unques-
tionably the means of inducing Professor Longfellow to send his prose and verse to the *Knickerbocker*,
of which his brother, Mr. Lewis Gaylord Clark, was
editor. A curious sample of the last, which I think
has hitherto escaped detection, will be found in the
Knickerbocker for January, 1835. Here it is:

THE SOUL.

AN EXTRACT FROM AN UNPUBLISHED POEM.

AND is this education ? This the training
    Of an immortal spirit for the skies ?
Would you, then, teach it virtue by restraining
    Its heavenward aspirations till it dies ?
Thus fit it for a life beyond the grave
    By making it a helot and a slave

To earth-born passions, and unholy lust,
    And grovelling appetites ? Oh! no. The soul
Blazoned with shame, and foul with earthly dust
    And for an emblem bearing o'er the whole
The crafty serpent, not the peaceful dove,
    Has no escutcheon for the courts above.

Why, then, prove false to Nature's noblest trust ?
Why, then, restrain the spirit's upward flight,
And make its dwelling in the loathsome dust,
  Until 'earth's shadow hath eclipsed its light' ?
Why deck the flesh, the sensual slave of sin,
And leave in rags the immortal guest within ?

Beware ! The Israelite of old who tore
  The lion in his path—when, poor and blind,
He saw the blessed light of heaven no more,
  Shorn of his nobler strength, and forced to grind
In prison, and at times led forth to be
A pander to Philistine revelry,

Destroyed himself, and with him those that made
  A cruel mockery of his sightless eyes!
So, too, the immortal soul, when once betrayed
  To minister to lusts it doth despise,
A poor blind slave, the scoff and jest of all,
Expires, and thousands perish in the fall !

I have not resurrected these dead bones to prove
that Mr. Longfellow sometimes wrote as indifferently
as lesser poets, but to point out the beginning of a
noble image in the last two stanzas of this abortive,
unfinished poem. It had a happy ending seven years
later in "Poems on Slavery." Let me give it here as
a lesson in the art of revision :

THE WARNING.

Beware! The Israelite of old, who tore
   The lion in his path—when, poor and blind,
He saw the blessed light of heaven no more,
   Shorn of his noble strength, and forced to grind
In prison, and at last led forth to be
A pander to Philistine revelry,

Upon the pillars of the temple laid
   His desperate hands, and in its overthrow
Destroyed himself, and with him those who made
   A cruel mockery of his sightless woe;
The poor, blind Slave, the scoff and jest of all,
Expired, and thousands perished in the fall !

There is a poor, blind Samson in this land,
   Shorn of his strength, and bound in bonds of steel,
Who may, in some grim revel, raise his hand,
   And shake the pillars of this Commonweal,
Till the vast Temple of our liberties
A shapeless mass of wreck and rubbish lies.

When "Outre-Mer," which appears to have failed
when issued in parts, was published in two volumes
by the Harpers in 1835, the genial critic of the
Knickerbocker remembered not to forget. "The
author of this work, in our opinion, has a glorious
career before him. With a mind pure and simple,
yet strong and ardent, and stored with learning, he

writes always as if under the influence of a true inspiration. As a scholar, especially in his acquaintance with modern languages, we believe Professor
Longfellow unequalled by any author of his years in
America or England. His style, which is peculiarly
his own, is polished and free, his moral ken is exquisite, his humor rich without rudeness, and keen
without asperity. With all the good old English
writers he is a familiar acquaintance, and, having
thumbed their black-letter tomes to some purpose,
he has saturated his mind with their refreshing
spirit." If the opinion of one who has thumbed
black-letter tomes, in a limited way, in libraries, and
who, if he has a familiar acquaintance with anything, has it with good old English literature,
should weigh in the scale, this was just what Mr.
Longfellow had not done.

A reasonable estimate of the Longfellow of this
period was reached by the *Athenæum* three years
later. Here is the gist of it, which I think was from
the pen of Henry Fothergill Chorley : " This writer
—not unknown here as the author of 'Outer-Mer'
—comes nearer to a literary character than most of
his associates. A professor of modern tongues in
Harvard University, it is said ; not of unknown
tongues, we presume, though we were just about to
call him an *Irvingite*. We speak in the literary ac-

ceptation, not theological. We cannot say that he
imitates the author of the 'Sketch-Book'; he has a
spirit of his own. But it seems to us that his mind
is much of the same description. He is sprightly,
and witty, and graphic; he has seen much of the
world and used his opportunities well. There is an
elegant ease in 'his style—finished, but not finical;
just the thing, as we say of a private gentleman
whose manners and dress excite no other remark,
while they satisfy all who observe them. And with-
al he has the genial *bonhomie* of Irving. He sees
the pleasant side of things. He likes that his reader
should be innocently pleased, and is content if he
be so. If Longfellow, in a word, had come before
Irving his fame would be that of a founder of a
school (so far as America is concerned) rather than
one of the scholars. As it is he may be popular, but
not famous, and will hardly have credit even for
what he is worth." Before leaving for his European tour Professor Longfellow married a daughter of
Judge Barrett Potter, of his native town. That is to
say, as nearly as I can make out, for he may have
met and married the young lady abroad. The shadow of his first great sorrow fell upon him at Rotterdam, where she passed suddenly into the world of
souls, and where, amid the plashing of its sluggish
waters, her dust is mouldering away.

Let me return to "Outre-Mer" long enough to give my early impression of it. It is (*me judice*) more scholarly than the "Sketch-Book," and the style is sweeter and mellower than Irving had yet attained; like Sidney, the writer warbled in poetic prose. Among the countries which he visited France awakened the deepest interest in him, and partook of his tenderest emotion, partly because he was deeply read in its literature, and partly because it was opulent in old-time picturesqueness. We find in the ninth chapter, which glances at "The Trouvères," the first two of his many French translations. One is a song in praise of Spring, by Charles d'Orléans, the other a copy of verses upon a sleeping child. They are elegantly rendered, but we feel in reading them (whether we know French or not) that the spirit of their originals has evaded Professor Longfellow, as it evaded Miss Costello, who published in the same year a volume of similar mistakes, which are redolent of the nineteenth but not of the fifteenth century. "Outre-Mer" will always possess a charm to the student of American literature as a rare example of a nondescript sort of prose—half narrative, half legendary, and wholly poetical—which ranks, and ought to rank, among the things which were. It will never flourish here again; but forty years ago it surprised and delighted literate and sympathetic

readers, to whom, and their children after them, it
unlocked the treasure-house of European travel, and
flung its jewels about lavishly.   It was the Old World
in the New World, with all its storied rivers and
mountains, its royal palaces, and parks, and cathedrals, its libraries and picture-galleries, and   its
peoples with their customs and literatures.   Quietly
humorous, prettily pathetic, pensive and imaginative, sentimental readers were drawn to the tiny
sketch of "Jacqueline," humorous readers to "Mar-
tin Franc and the Monks of St. Anthony" and "The
Notary of Périgueux," and bookish readers to "The
Trouvères," "Ancient Spanish Ballads," and "The
Devotional Poetry," with which the admirers of
"Coplas de Manrique" were already familiar.   Writing in May, 1882, I cannot say that "Outre-Mer" is
a remarkable volume ; but remembering what American literature was in 1835, I see that it was an important book then ; that it fairly won all the praise
it received ; that it eminently represented the talents
and the genius of its writer; and that it mapped out
his future career as if by inspiration.   The reputation of Professor Longfellow was so assured at this
time that he was selected by the faculty of Harvard
University to succeed Mr. George Ticknor, who re-
signed his professorship of modern languages and literature.   He gave up his chair at Bowdoin, and went

abroad again to continue and finish his studies in the literature of Northern Europe. A summer in Denmark and Sweden and an autumn and winter in Germany consumed little more than a year. The death of Mrs. Longfellow at Rotterdam arrested his studies and his travel until the following spring and summer, which were passed in the Tyrol and Switzerland. He returned to the United States in November, 1836, and entered upon his duties at Harvard.

I have now completed the circle which started with Mr. Longfellow's note of April 20, 1878, and I have before me the book to which he there referred. I violate no confidence when I say that the paper devoted to Mr. Longfellow in "Homes of American Authors" is from the brilliant and versatile pen of Mr. George William Curtis. Mr. Curtis was the life-long friend of Mr. Longfellow, and the accuracy of what he wrote about him and his surroundings may be depended upon. I shall use the substance of it in what follows, either in his words or my own, as may seem best.

One calm afternoon in the summer of 1837 a young gentleman of thirty sauntered from the high-road of Cambridge down the elm-shaded walk that led to the old Craigie House. Gaining the door, he halted suddenly to study the huge, old-fashioned brass knocker and the quaint handle that bespoke familiarity

with things Colonial and Revolutionary. These, of
course, were not without their charm to this travelled
student, who must have seen the like many times over
in England and Holland ; but it was not this that de-
tained him there, let us fancy with his hat uplifted,
and the wind rippling through his hair. It was not
antiquity but memory that held him fast—the memory of a soldier and a statesman whom the world
admires and reveres—Washington. Hither he came
with his army after the lost battle of Bunker Hill—
stalwart farmers' sons in ragged regimentals, bronzed
at the plough and in the hay-field, scarred in Indian
wars, indomitable—and drilling them, along the road,
and in the green pastures, Harvard students, professors of learned tongues and the humane arts, doctors,
lawyers, and a host of fighting parsons baptized with
fire at Lexington and Concord. He thought of the
great Commander. "Had his hand, perhaps, lifted
this same latch, lingering as he clasped it in a whirl
of emotions ? Had he, too, paused in the calm summer afternoon, and watched the silver gleam of the
broad river in the meadows, the dreamy blue of the
Milton hills beyond ? And had the tranquillity of
that landscape penetrated his heart with 'the sleep
that is among the hills,' and whose fairest dream to
him was a hope now realized in the peaceful prosper-
ity of his country ? "

"The dreamer upraised the huge brass knocker, which fell with a heavy clang. A servant appeared as the wide door opened, and invited the visitor to enter. He bowed and asked for Mrs. Craigie. The door of a little parlor was opened softly, and that lady appeared—a tall, erect figure, crowned with a majestic turban, such as our stately grandmothers delighted to wear, and calmly surveyed him with keen gray eyes. Everything about her bespoke the gentlewoman of a past generation. To an inquiry of the young gentleman, who bent his manliness before her widowhood, she gravely answered : 'But I lodge students no longer.' 'But I am not a student; I am a Professor in the University.' 'A Professor?' she demanded, with perhaps a shade of incredulity. 'Professor Longfellow,' he added, thus introducing himself. 'Ah! that is different. I will show you what there is.'" What is that which she seems to hear before her? Only the ticking clock, which says: "This is the master of the house—the master, master." There are spirits about you, Mrs. Craigie. "Thereupon she preceded the Professor up the stairs, and, gaining the upper hall, paused at each door, opened it, permitted him to perceive its delightful fitness for his purpose—kindled expectation to the utmost—then quietly closed the door again, observing, 'You cannot have that.' It was most Barmecide hospitality.

The professorial eyes glanced restlessly around the fine old-fashioned points of the mansion, marked the wooden carvings, the air of opulent respectability in the past—which corresponds in New England to the impression of ancient nobility in old England—and wondered in which of these pleasant fields of suggestive association he was to be allowed to pitch his tent. The turbaned hostess at length opened the door of the southeast corner room in the second story, and while the guest looked wistfully in, and awaited the customary 'You cannot have that,' he was agreeably surprised by a variation of the strain to the effect that he might occupy it. The room was upon the front of the house, and looked over the meadows to the river. It had an atmosphere of fascinating repose, in which the young man was at once domesticated as in an old home. The elms of the avenue shaded his windows, and as he glanced from them the summer lay asleep upon the landscape in the windless day. 'This,' said the old lady, with a slight sadness in her voice, as if speaking of times for ever past and to which she herself properly belonged—'this was General Washington's chamber!'"

Professor Longfellow was housed as a poet should be—in a noble mansion, in the shadows of immemorial elms, and in the midst of a pastoral landscape. "The traveller upon the high-road before the Craigie House, even if he knew nothing of its story, would be struck by its quaint dignity and respectability, and make a legend, if he could not find one already made. If, however, his lot had been cast in Cambridge, and he had been able to secure a room in the mansion, he would not rest until he had explored the traditions of its origin and occupancy, and had given his fancy moulds in which to run its images. He would have found in the churchyard of Cambridge a freestone tablet, supported by five pillars, upon which, with the name Col. John Vassal, died in 1747, are sculptured the words Vas-sol and the emblems, a goblet and sun. Whether this device was a proud assertion of the fact that the fortunes of the family should be always as

'A beaker full of the warm South,'

happily no historian records; for the beaker has long since been drained to the dregs, and of the stately family nothing survived in the early part of the Poet's residence in the house but an old black man who had been born, a slave, in the mansion during the last days of the Vassals, and who occasionally returned to visit his earliest haunts, like an Indian the hunting-grounds of his extinct tribe. This Col. John Vassal is supposed to have built the house towards the close of the first half of the last century. Upon an iron in

the back of one of the chimneys there is the date
1759, which probably commemorates no more than
the fact of its own insertion at that period, inas-
much as the builder of the house would hardly
commit the authentic witness of its erection to the
mercies of smoke and soot. History capitulates before the exact date of the building of the Craigie
House as completely as before that of the foundation
of Thebes. But the house was evidently generously
built, and Col. John Vassal, having lived there in generous style, died, and lies under the freestone tablet.
His son John fell upon revolutionary times, and
was a royalist. The observer of the house will not
be surprised at the fact. That the occupant of such
a mansion should, in colonial troubles, side with the
government was as natural as the fealty of a Doug-
las or a Howard to the king. The house, however,
passed from his hands, and was purchased by the
provincial government at the beginning of serious
work with the mother-country. After the battle of
Bunker Hill it was allotted to General Washington
as his headquarters. It was entirely unfurnished,
but the charity of neighbors filled it with necessary
furniture. The southeastern room upon the lower
floor, at the right of the front door, and now occupied
as a study by Mr. Longfellow, was devoted to the
same purpose by Washington. The room over it, as

Madame Craigie has already informed us, was his chamber. The room upon the lower floor, in the rear of the study, which was afterwards enlarged, and is now the Poet's library, was occupied by the aids-de-camp of the commander-in-chief. And the southwest room upon the lower floor was Mrs. Washington's drawing-room. The rich old wood-carving in this apartment is still remarkable, still certifies the frequent presence of fine society. For, although during the year in which Washington occupied the mansion there could have been as little desire as means for gay festivity, yet Washington and his leading associates were all gentlemen—men who would have graced the elegance of a court with the same dignity that made the plainness of a republic admirable. Many of Washington's published letters are dated from this house. And could the walls whisper, we should hear more and better things of him than could ever be recorded. In his chamber are still the gay-painted tiles peculiar to fine houses of the period ; and upon their quaint and grotesque images the glancing eyes of the Poet's children now wonderingly linger, where the sad and doubtful ones of Washington must have often fallen as he meditated the darkness of the future. Many of these peculiarities and memories of the mansion appear in the Poet's verses. In the opening of the poem 'To a Child' the tiles are painted anew :

'The lady with the gay macaw,
    The dancing girl, the grave Bashaw
        With bearded lip and chin ;
    And, leaning idly o'er his gate,
    Beneath the imperial fan of state,
        The Chinese mandarin.'

"The next figure that distinctly appears in the old
house is that of Thomas Tracy, a personage of whom
the household traditions are extremely fond. He was
a rich man in the fabulous style of the East—such a
nabob as Oriental imaginations can everywhere easily
conjure, while practical experience wonders that they
are so rare. He carried himself with a rare lavish-
ness. Servants drank costly wines from carved
pitchers in the incredible days of Thomas Tracy;
and in his stately mansion a hundred guests sat down
to banquets, and pledged their host in draughts
whose remembrances keep his name sweet, as royal
bodies were preserved in wine and spices. In the
early days of national disorder he sent out privateers
to scour the seas, and bleed Spanish galleons of
their sunniest juices, and reap golden harvests of
fruits and spices, of silks and satins, from East and
West Indian ships, that the bountiful table of Vassal House might not fail, nor the carousing days
of Thomas Tracy become credible. But these 'spacious times' of the large-hearted and large-handed

gentleman suddenly ended. The wealthy man failed; no more hundred guests appeared at banquets; no more privateers sailed into Boston Bay, reeking with riches from every zone; Spain, the Brazils, the Indies no more rolled their golden sands into the pockets of Thomas Tracy; servants, costly wines, carved pitchers, all began to glimmer and go, and finally Thomas Tracy and his incredible days vanished as entirely as the gorgeous pavilions with which the sun in setting piles the summer west.

"After this illuminated chapter in the history of the house Captain Joseph Lee, a brother of Madame Tracy, appears in the annals, but does not seem to have illustrated them by any special gifts or graces. Tradition remains silent, pining for Thomas Tracy, until it lifts its head upon the entry into the house of Andrew Craigie, apothecary-general to the Northern provincial army, who amassed a fortune in that office, which, like his great predecessor, he presently lost, but not until he had built a bridge over the Charles River, connecting Cambridge with Boston, which is still known by his name. Andrew Craigie did much for the house, even enlarging it to its present form; but tradition is hard upon him. It declares that he was a huge man, heavy and dull, and evidently looks upon his career as the high lyric of Thomas Tracy's, muddled into tough prose. In the best and

most prosperous days of Andrew Craigie the estate
comprised two hundred acres. Upon the site of the
present observatory, not far from the mansion, stood
a summer house, but whether of any rare architectural device whether, in fact, any orphic genius of
those days 'said' a summer house, which, like that of
Mr. Emerson's, only lacked 'scientific arrangement'
to be quite perfect does not appear. Like the apo
thecary to the Northern army, the summer house is
gone, as likewise an aqueduct that brought water a
quarter of a mile. Tradition, so enamored of Tracy,
is generous enough to mention a dinner party given
by Andrew Craigie every Saturday, and on one occasion points out peruked and powdered Talleyrand
among the guests. This betrays the presence in the
house of the best society then to be had. But the
prosperous Craigie could not avoid the fate of his
opulent predecessor, who also gave banquets. Things
rushed on too rapidly for him. The bridge, aqueduct,
and summer house, two hundred acres and an enlarged house, were too much for the fortune acquired in
dealing medicaments to the Northern army. The
'spacious times' of Andrew Craigie also came to an
end. A visitor walked with him through his large
and handsome rooms, and, struck with admiration,
exclaimed : 'Mr. Craigie, I should think you would
lose yourself in all this spaciousness.'   'Mr.' (tradi-

tion has forgotten the name), said the hospitable and ruined host, 'I *have* lost myself in it,' and we do not find him again.

"After his disappearance Mrs. Craigie, bravely swallowing the risings of pride, and still revealing in her character and demeanor the worthy mistress of a noble mansion, let rooms. Edward Everett resided here just after his marriage, and while still Professor in the college of which he was afterwards President. Willard Phillips, Jared Sparks, now the head of the University, and Joseph E. Worcester, the Lexicographer, have all resided here, sometimes sharing the house with Mrs. Craigie, and, in the case of Mr. Worcester, occupying it jointly with Mr. Longfellow when the grave old lady removed her stately turban for the last time." Such was Craigie House, its traditions, and early dwellers, as they were repeated and painted by Mr. Curtis about thirty years ago.

The letters of Charles Sumner, who was connected by friendship and intermarriage with Mr. Longfellow, are sprinkled with allusions to his poetic neighbor. For example, in a letter to Dr. Lieber, at New York, dated from Boston on November 17, 1836, he writes : "Longfellow has returned home, having arrived only three days ago, full of pleasant reminiscences and of health. He tells me that he called upon Mittermaier with a letter from you. He is a

very pleasant fellow, and will at once assume the
charge of Ticknor's department." We learn a little
further on that he left the Appletons in Switzerland.
This brings me to a meeting between Mr. Longfellow
and Mr. Samuel Ward at the house of Herr Adolph
Zimmern, the banker of the latter, at Heidelberg, on
an evening in March, 1836. There were present besides Mr. Ward and his man of millions Mrs. William Cullen Bryant and her young daughter, and
Professor Henry Wadsworth Longfellow. The Port-
lander and the New-Yorker adjourned early to the
hotel of the latter, the Badischer Hof, where they
talked until daybreak, of how Tieck used to read to
them his admirable translations of Shakespeare, and
poems by Uhland and the old balladists, and how he
told them of the noble rendering of Dante by Prince
John of Saxony. The next day Mr. Ward went to
the rooms of his late-and-early-talking friend, which
were strewn with books, and were situated in a house
on the main street with a view of the castle in the
near distance. More and later talk over bottles of
Rhine wine. Two days afterwards these *bons cama-
rades* started for the town of Treves, the younger
dropping behind at Mannheim.

The reputation of Professor Longfellow began in
the *Knickerbocker* for September, 1838. Its germ
was this :

A PSALM OF LIFE.

WHAT THE HEART OF THE YOUNG MAN SAID TO THE
PSALMIST.

" Life that shall send
A challenge to its end,
And when it comes say, ' Welcome, friend !'"

The summer before it appeared Mr. Ward visited the room of his young crony. It was at the Astor, in the fourth story, and was empty. Not exactly, for there was a poem there, probably "A Psalm of Life," which chanted itself into the soul of Willis and the purse of Lewis Gaylord Clark. Never since young Drake and Halleck had stirred New York to the deeps was there such a commotion. It passed from Halleck to Washington Irving, from the two to King, the editor of the *American*, and to Dr. Hawks, and from these to high and low. It did *not* pass to Mr. Edgar Allan Poe, who was on the eve of moving from Arch Street, Philadelphia, into a new house, and was on the point of running his critical stiletto into Mr. Washington Irving. "A Psalm of Life" was a dirge of death to him, for he hated the psalmist, as he showed in the pages of the *Gentleman's Magazine*, of which he was soon to be Sylvanus Unurban. Here is what he wrote about "Voices

of the Night": "In looking over a file of news-
papers not long ago our attention was arrested by
the opening lines of a few stanzas headed 'Hymn
to the Night.' We read them again and again, and,
although some blemishes were readily discoverable,
we bore them away in memory with the firm belief
that a poet of high genius had at length arisen
amongst us, and with the resolve to so express our
opinion at the first opportunity which should offer.
The perusal of the entire volume now presented to
the public by the author of this 'Hymn to the
Night' has not, indeed, greatly modified our impressions in regard to that particular poem, not
greatly even in regard to the genius of the poet,
but very greatly in respect to his capacity for the
ultimate achievement of any well-founded monument, any enduring reputation. Our general conclusion is one similar to that which 'Hyperion' induced, and which we stated of late in a concise notice
of that book. The author has in one or two points
ability, and in these one or two points that ability
regards the very brightest qualities of the poetical
soul. His imagination, for example, is vivid ; and in
saying thus how much do we say ! But he appears
to us singularly deficient in all those important facul-
ties which give artistical form, and without which
never was immortality effected. He has no combin-

ing or binding force. He has absolutely nothing of unity.

"His brief pieces (to whose brevity he has been led by an instinct of the deficiencies we now note) abound in high thoughts, either positively insulated, or showing these same deficiencies by the recherché spirit of their connection. And thus his productions are scintillations from the highest poetical truth, rather than this highest truth itself. By truth, here, we mean that perfection which is the result only of the strictest proportion and adaptation in all the poetical requisites—these requisites being considered as each existing in the highest degree of beauty and strength." This reads a little severely, but is mild beside the next paragraph, which was written shortly before it by the same incisive pen : "Were it possible to thrust into a bag the lofty thought and manner of the 'Pilgrims of the Rhine,' together with the quirks and quibbles and true humor of 'Tristram Shandy,' not forgetting a few of the heartier drolleries of Rabelais and one or two of the Phantasy Pieces of the Lorrainean Callot, the whole, when well shaken up, and thrown out, would be a very tolerable imitation of 'Hyperion.' This may appear to be commendation, but we do not intend it as such. Works like this of Professor Longfellow are the triumphs of Tom o' Bed-

lam and the grief of all true criticism. They are
potent in unsettling the popular faith in Art—a
faith which at no day more than the present needed
the support of men of letters. That such things
succeed at all is attributable to the fact that there
exist men of genius who now and then, unmindful
of duty, indite them—that men of genius *ever* indite
them is attributable to the fact that they are often
the most indolent of human beings. A man of true
talent who would demur at the great labor requisite
for the stern demands of high art—at that unre-
mitting toil and patient elaboration which, when
soul-guided, result in Beauty, Unity, Totality, and
Truth—men, we say, who would demur at such
labor make no scruple of scattering at random a
profusion of rich thought in the pages of such far-
ragoes as 'Hyperion.' Here, indeed, there is little
trouble, but even that little is most unprofitably lost.
To the writers of these things we say—all Ethics
lie, and all History lies, or the world shall forget
ye and your *works*. We have no design of com-
menting, at any length, upon what Professor Longfellow has written. We are indignant that he, too,
has been recreant to the good cause. We, therefore, dismiss his 'Hyperion' in brief. We grant
him high qualities, but deny him *the Future*. In
the present instance, without design, without shape,

without beginning, middle, or end, what earthly object has his book accomplished? What definite impression has it left?"

Let me present here, as the reverse of the Poe medal, an old, tattered letter which explains itself:

"CAMBRIDGE, Dec. 7, 1839.

"MY DEAR OLLAPOD: I hope this letter will find you in better health than when your last dateless epistle was written. You were then on the point of starting for New York and Albany. Have you got back again to Philadelphia, or did you not go out of its lovely gates? I felt quite startled at the account you gave of your health. Why did you refuse to go to Santa Cruz? You could have taken Willie or have left him with your brother. I think you were wrong. It would have been a delightful excursion. I hope you will think better of it and go, even now. It will not do for you to sit at home and grieve your soul away. Your Autumnal Dirge is one of the most sweetly solemn poems I ever read. There is the difference of writing from the *heart* and from the *imagination* merely. In that poem I recognize my friend in his better hours. I got Clapp to publish it, with two or three lines introducing it, in his paper. The piece is much admired here.

"I am glad you find something good in 'Hyperion,' and trust that you will likewise find something to like in 'Voices of the Night,' which I shall send you next week, though there will be very little in the volume which you have not seen before.

"On the next page you will find two Literary Notices, which I wish you would publish and send me a copy thereof. I think Menzel's book will delight you vastly. Take my word for it. Spencer you have probably heard of before!

"Now, Clark, don't let such an age pass before you write again. I never see your paper nor your handwriting nowadays. I sometimes think you have taken offence at something, yet cannot really believe so, but have put it down to *multifariousness* and ill-health.

"Very truly yours, as ever,

"HENRY WAD. LONGFELLOW."

To show Mr. Longfellow's kindness I will give here the substance of two little notes which he wrote to me in November and December, 1871. They referred to a young person who had recently emigrated to the United States, I have no doubt for good and sufficient reasons. He wrote and spoke several languages indifferently, English not being one of them; sang some, and drew a great deal, especially at the long bow; was rather at sea in regard to property, personal, literary, and other; remembered to forget when he passed off a German translation for an American original, stating under precisely what circumstances he happened to write it, and with the strongest and most impudent determination to be—he was already—a man of letters. This cool youth Mr.

Longfellow took the liberty of introducing to me, though he had not the honor of his personal acquaintance. He brought him a letter of introduction from an English lady of rank, and he was anxious to aid him in his plans. He wished to write for the periodicals, and Mr. Longfellow ventured to ask from me a friendly hearing for him. My friendly hearing, which would have been given any way, put a few shekels into his pockets, and put Mr. Longfellow to the trouble of writing again to me. He was obliged to me for what I had done, and his *protégé* had written to him to express his gratification for my kindness. He enclosed the letter of introduction which induced him to appeal to me in his despair of doing anything for him there. Would I be so kind as to return the letter after I had read it? If Master Nameless could not make his way in New York with the start I had given him, he should despair of his success in the line he had chosen. With great regard and many thanks, he was mine faithfully. I have also before me another note from the pen of this genial gentleman, written in the early autumn of 1850, and addressed to a Southern man of letters who was stopping at the Revere House. He hopes that this child of the South will come out to Cambridge as early as he can, that he may have the pleasure of introducing him to any gentleman that he might like

to know there, and still have time to drive to Mount
Auburn. He hopes also that he will do him the fa-
vor to dine with him, and he will order dinner early,
so that he may have ample time for the afternoon
for Springfield, if he still adhered to his plan of
going that way. And he was his faithfully. The
Shadow cloaked from head to foot has borne both
away, one to the cemetery at Richmond that over-
looks the winding James, the other to Mount Auburn
and his own river of song—the Charles.

> " And did you once see Shelley plain,
>   And did he stop and speak to you ?
>   And did you speak to him again ?
>   How strange it seems, and new !"

The mention of "Hyperion" and "Voices of the
Night" sends me back to Charles Sumner, who addressed a letter from London to Mr. George S. Hillard, of Boston, on March 18, 1840 : " I have just
found Longfellow's 'Hyperion,' and shall sit up all
night to devour it. I have bought up all the copies
of 'Voices of the Night' in London to give to my
friends." Two years later Mr. Sumner wrote from
Boston to his brother George : "I cannot forbear saying how much pleasure it gave me to see your few
words about Longfellow. He cares not at all for
politics or statistics, for the Syrian question or the

disasters of Afghanistan. But to him the magnificent world of literature and Nature is open ; every
beauty of sentiment and truth and language has for
him a relish ; and every heart that feels is sure of a
response from him. I feel for his genius and worth
the greatest reverence, as for him personally the
warmest love." Sumner's letters, always charming,
are never more charming than when they follow the
fortunes of his friend, whom they bring before us
continually. One would like to know when he finally became Master of Craigie House. Sumner shall
tell us, speaking from Cambridge on May 9, 1841 :
"Once again from the headquarters of our great
chief. Since I last wrote you Mrs. Craigie, the widow of the builder of Craigie's Bridge and the own-
er of this house, has died and been removed from
the spacious rooms to a narrow bed at Mount Auburn." He shall also tell us, as he told him, about
the usefulness of his poems, in a letter from London
in the autumn of 1842 : " A few days ago an old
classmate, upon whom the world had not smiled,
came to my office to prove some debts before me in
bankruptcy. While writing the formal parts of the
paper I inquired about his reading and the books
which interested him now (I believe that he has been
a great reader). He said that he read very little ;
that he hardly found anything that was written from

the heart and was really true. 'Have you read Longfellow's "Hyperion"?' I said. 'Yes,' he replied,
'and I admire it very much. I think it is a very
great book.' He then added, in a very solemn manner: 'I think I may say that Longfellow's "Psalm
of Life" saved me from suicide. I first found it on
a scrap of newspaper, in the hands of two Irishwo-
men, soiled and worn, and I was at once touched by
it.' Think, my dear friend, of this soul into which
you have poured the waters of life. Such a tribute
is higher than the words of Rogers, much as I value
them."

Two brief extracts from Sumner's letters shall con-
clude what I have to say about Longfellow's life at
Craigie House at this time. He is writing to Mr.
John Jay, of New York, from Boston, on May 25,
1843: "If you and Mrs. Jay should visit Boston—
perhaps Nahant may be an attraction in the heats of
summer—we all count upon renewing our acquaintance with you. You will probably find Longfellow
a married man, for he is now engaged to Miss Fanny
Appleton—the Mary Ashburton of 'Hyperion' —a
lady of the greatest sweetness, imagination, and elevation of character, with the most striking personal
charms." About two months later he writes to
Dr. Lieber: " Longfellow is to be happy for a
fortnight in the shades of Cambridge, then to visit

his wife's friends in Berkshire, then his own. I am all *alone—alone.* My friends fall away from me.''

The extravagance of Mr. Sumner's opinion of Mr. Longfellow's poetry leads me to observe that I have wandered too far away from it ; so, without more ado, I will go back to where I was when I began to track him through this labyrinth of reminiscence. His first literary labors in Craigie House, as nearly as I can make out, were a paper on "Frithiof's Saga," and another on his friend Hawthorne's ''Twice-told Tales," both of which were published in the *North American* in 1837.· It is to his honor as well as his sagacity that he was among the earliest to dis-cover and proclaim the excellence of Hawthorne's imaginative stories and essays. These papers were followed during the next year by one upon "Anglo-Saxon Literature," and a second upon " Paris in the Seventeenth Century." If they are pleasant reading for leisure moments after the lapse of forty years— and they certainly are—they were much better read-ing when the dew and the bloom were upon them. For, without boasting in regard to our familiarity with other literatures than our own, there can be no manner of doubt that our ancestors knew much less about them than we do ; there can also be no manner of doubt that our earliest knowledge of German literature is largely due to the writings of Professor Long-fellow. The first Englishman to transplant the wild flowers and wilder weeds of the German garden into the parterres of England was the Mr. Benjamin Thompson who translated "The Stranger" of Kotze-bue—that lugubrious, sentimental melodrama which drenched with hot tears the handkerchiefs of our grandmothers (possibly our own, likewise, in the green and salad days), which Sheridan declared that he had written every word of, and in which the Foth-eringay was so magnificent, as poor Pendennis found to his cost. Mr. Thompson was succeeded by Mr. Coleridge, two years afterwards, with a spirited but loose rendering of Schiller's "Wallenstein," and he by Mr. Lewis with wonder-tales and other *diablerie* for the closet and the stage and hysteria, whose read-ing of "Faust" to Shelley resulted in that glorious fragment of a translation of his, and indirectly re-sulted in Byron's "Deformed Transformed." They came in troops and battalions—forgotten translators of indifferent German into bad English: Gillies, De Quincey, and Carlyle, who represented scholarly waste, opiates, and dyspeptic eccentricity. The glory of first scattering a largesse of German fancy and feeling in the New World belongs to Henry Wads-worth Longfellow. The papers that I have enume-rated were written, or finished, at Craigie House, as well as a series of others descriptive of travel in Germany and Switzerland, through which, like a silken string through a rosary of beads, ran a slight personal story, half real, half imaginative, and throughout poetic. It concerned itself with the life-history of Paul Flemming, a tender-hearted, rather shadowy young gentleman, who had lost the friend of his youth and had gone abroad, that the sea might be between him and the grave. "Alas! between him and his sorrow there could be no sea but that of time." He loitered from place to place, noting what hit his sensitive fancy, and prattling about men and women and books—pilgrim, student, and dreamer. The hand that had penned "Outre-Mer" was visible in every word of "Hyperion," but the hand had grown firmer in the Craigie House than it was at Bowdoin, and the learned sympathies of the penman had embraced the singularities of a richer literature than that of old Spain and old France. Dismissing the romantic element of "Hyperion" for what it is worth (and there must have been genuine worth in it, since it was the cause of its immediate popularity), the chief and permanent value of the book lay in the new element of German fantasy and romanticism which it poured into American letters. It would have come in time, without doubt, but to Professor Longfellow belongs the honor of having hastened the time and ushered in the dawn. He was the herald of German Poetry in the New World. The second book of "Hyperion" contains, I believe, his first published translations from the German—the "Whither?" of Müller. The third book contains "The Black Knight," "The Castle by the Sea," "The Song of the Silent Land," and "Beware!" Besides these translations in verse there is, in the first book, a chapter on "Jean Paul, the Only One," and in the second book a chapter on "Goethe," whom Mr. Paul Flemming does not greatly admire. His friend, the Baron, defends the old heathen by saying that he is an artist and copies nature. "So did the artists who made the bronze lamps of Pompeii. Would you hang one of those in your hall? To say that a man is an artist and copies nature is not enough. There are two great schools of art—the imitative and the imaginative. The latter is the more noble and the more enduring."

The dignity of the literary profession was earnestly maintained by Mr. Longfellow. "I do not see," said the Baron, in one of his conversations with Paul Flemming—"I do not see why a successful book is not as great an event as a successful campaign, only different in kind, and not easily compared." The lives of literary men are melancholy pictures of man's strength and weakness, and on that very ac-

count, he thought, were profitable for encouragement, consolation, and warning. "And after all,"
continued Flemming, "perhaps the greatest lesson
which the lives of literary men teach us is told in a
single word: Wait! Every man must patiently bide
his time. He must wait. More particularly in lands
like my native land, where the pulse of life beats
with such feverish and impatient throbs, is the lesson needful. Our national character wants the dignity of repose. We seem to live in the midst of a
battle—there is such a din, such a hurrying to and
fro. In the streets of a crowded city it is difficult
to walk slowly. You feel the rushing of the crowd,
and rush with it onward. In the press of our life
it is difficult to be calm. In this stress of wind and
tide, all professions seem to drag their anchors and
are swept out into the main. The voices of the Present say, 'Come!' But the voices of the Past say,
'Wait!' With calm and solemn footsteps the rising tide bears against the rushing torrent up stream,
and pushes back the hurrying waters. With no less
calm and solemn footsteps, nor less certainty, does
a great mind bear up against public opinion and
push back its hurrying stream. Therefore should
every man wait—should bide his time. Not in listless idleness, not in useless pastime, not in queru-
lous dejection, but in constant, steady, cheerful en-

deavors, always willing and fulfilling, and accomplishing his task, that, when the occasion comes, he may be equal to the occasion. And if it never comes, what matters it? What matters it to the world whether I, or you, or another man did such a deed or wrote such a book, so be it the deed and book were well done? It is the part of an indiscreet and troublesome ambition to care too much about fame, about what the world says of us ; to be always looking into the faces of others for approval ; to be always anxious for the effect of what we do and say ; to be always shouting to hear the echo of our own voices. If you look about you, you will see men who are wearing life away in feverish anxiety of fame, and the last we shall ever hear of them will be the funeral bell that tolls them to their early graves! Unhappy men, and unsuccessful! because their purpose is, not to accomplish well their task, but to clutch the 'trick and fantasy of fame' ; and they go to their graves with purposes unaccomplished and wishes unfulfilled. Better for them, and for the world in their example, had they known how to wait! Believe me, the talent of success is nothing more than doing what you can do well, and doing well whatever you do, without a thought of fame. If it come at all, it will come because it is deserved, not because it is sought after. And, moreover, there will be no misgivings, no disappointment, no hasty, feverish, exhausting excitement.''

If fame comes because it is deserved, which may or may not be true, assuredly it comes to some much sooner than to others—much sooner to the Byrons than the Wordsworths, the Longfellows than the Hawthornes—why, their contemporaries and rivals do not perceive as clearly as those who come after them. Poor Mr. Poe could never understand why Mr. Longfellow was a more successful writer than he was. He might have discovered the reason, however, if he had looked for it, since it lay upon the surface of the American character. Our ideals were not lofty forty years ago, nor are they very lofty now. But then, as now, we knew what we wanted in song and art, and we thought we could distinguish what was new from what was old. We knew what to expect from our poets. Bryant was calm, meditative, philosophic; Willis, when not modishly Scriptural, was light and airy; Halleck, spirited and martial; Pierpont, occasional and moral—a few epithets described them, and others who were not worthy to rank with them. We recognized their excellence, but it by no means exhausted our admiration and capacity for greater excellence. There was—there always is—room for a new poet, though old poets, and old critics, and old readers are generally slow to ad-

mit the fact. There were fertile gardens which yielded our elder singers no flowers—gardens in which no
seed of theirs had ever been sown, or, having been
sown, had refused to germinate. I scarcely know
how to describe the seed which Professor Longfellow
began to scatter in " Hyperion" and " Voices of the
Night." Romanticism does not describe it, for there
is nothing romantic in "The Hymn to the Night " ;
nor does morality describe it, except, perhaps, as it
bourgeoned in " A Psalm of Life." The lesson of the
last was the lesson of endurance, and patience, and
cheerfulness. It had been taught by other poets,
but not as this one taught it—not in verse that set
itself to music in the memory of thousands, and in
words that were pictures. The young man who wrote
"A Psalm of Life" possessed the art of saying
things, and a very rare art it is. Shakespeare possessed it in a supreme degree, and Pope and Gray in a
greater measure than greater poets. Merciless critics
have pointed out flaws in the literary workmanship
of " A Psalm of Life," but its readers never saw
them, or, seeing them, never cared for them. They
found it a hopeful, helpful poem. "Footsteps of
Angels" is to me the most satisfactory of all these
nocturnal melodies. There is an indescribable tenderness in it, and the vision of the poet's dead wife
gliding into his chamber with noiseless footsteps,

taking a vacant chair beside him, and laying her hand in his, is very pathetic. "The Beleaguered City" is a product of poetic artifice of which there are but few examples in English poetry. It appears to have been compounded after a recipe which called for equal parts of outward fact and inward meaning. Given a material city, a river, a fog, and so on, the poet sets his wits to work to discover what corresponds, or can be made to correspond, with them spiritually. If he is skilful he constructs an ingenious poem of doubtful intellectual value. "Midnight Mass for the Dying Year" is a medley of mediæval suggestion and Shakespearean remembrance which demands a large and imaginative appreciation. The Shakespearean element seems to me out of place, though it adds to its impressiveness and effect as a whole. It is a medley, however, as I have said, and it must be judged by its own fantastic laws. Whatever faults disfigured "Voices of the Night" were lost sight of, or forgiven, for the sake of the beauties, and for the admirable poetic spirit which these beauties displayed. Such substantially is what I wrote four years ago, after re-reading the poems in question, and after mature deliberation, and I cannot depart from it now.

The growing popularity of Mr. Longfellow was hateful to the jealous spirit of Mr. Poe, who accused

him of plagiarizing from Tennyson in his "Midnight
Mass for the Dying Year," and from himself in "The
Beleaguered City." He emphasized the last charge
in a note to the Reverend Rufus Wilmot Griswold
under the date of March 22 (1841). Dr. Griswold
was about to publish his "Poets of America," and
Mr. Poe, who naturally desired to see himself among
them, sent him what he considered his best poems,
one or two of which he would be proud to see in his
book. "The one called 'The Haunted Palace' is
that of which I spoke in reference to Professor Longfellow's plagiarism. I first published the 'H. P.' in
Brooks's Museum, a monthly journal of Baltimore,
now dead. Afterwards I embodied it in a tale called
'The House of Usher,' in *Burton's Magazine*. Here
it was, I suppose, that Professor Longfellow saw it;
for about six weeks afterwards there appeared in the
Southern Literary Messenger a poem by him called
'The Beleaguered City,' which may be found in his
volume. The identity in title is striking, for by
'The Haunted Palace' I mean to imply a mind
haunted by phantoms—a disordered brain; and by
'The Beleaguered City' Prof. L. means just the
same. But the whole tournure of the poem is based
upon mine, as you will see at once. Its allegorical
conduct, the style of its versification and expression
—all are mine." I have just re-read "The Haunted

Palace " and " The Beleaguered City," with a view
to substantiating or refuting Mr. Poe's charge of
plagiarism against Mr. Longfellow, and, for the life of
me, I can find nothing in it. It was either the delu-
sion of a disordered brain, such as they both celebrated, or it was the weak invention of an enemy.
There was a mountain in Macedon, and a mountain in
Wales, and Poe's was—*Nascitur monte ridiculus
mus.* But the ingenious Mr. Poe was not alone in
depreciating Professor Longfellow ; for Miss Marga-
ret Fuller, as able, and honest, and conscientious a
gentlewoman as ever wielded the goose-quill in any
country, shared his heretical opinions, and promul-
gated her critical censure at a later period. Let me
give here the *précis* of this censure, as I find it in
her " Papers on Literature and Art," and as it probably appeared in the New York *Tribune.* My notes
are not so clear as I could wish, but I believe they
represent the words—they certainly do the thoughts
—of Miss Fuller. I cannot be sure of the order of
their succession : " We must confess to a coolness
towards Mr. Longfellow in consequence of the ex-
aggerated praises that have been bestowed upon him.
When we see a person of moderate powers receive
honors which should be reserved for the highest, we
feel somewhat like assailing him, and taking from
him the crown which should be reserved for grander

brows. And yet this is, perhaps, ungenerous. It
may be that the management of publishers, the hy-
perbole of paid or undiscriminating reviewers, or
some accidental cause which gives a temporary interest to productions beyond what they would permanently command, have raised such an one to a place
as much above his wishes as his claims, and which he
would rejoice, with honorable modesty, to vacate at
the approach of a worthier. We the more readily
believe this of Mr. Longfellow, as one so sensible of
the beauties of other writers, and so largely indebted
to them, *must* know his comparative rank better than
his readers have known it for him. So much adula-
tion is dangerous, for he is so lauded on all hands
that he is now able to collect his poems, which have
so widely circulated in previous volumes, and been
paid for so handsomely by the handsomest annu-
als, and have them illustrated by the most distinguished of our younger artists, and has found a flat-
terer in that very artist." Miss Fuller strenuously
objected to the portrait, especially the eyes, which
had an expression thrown into them that the original
lacked, and which made the rest of the face look
more weak, suggesting the idea of a dandy Pindar.
"Such is not the case with Mr. Longfellow himself.
He is not a Pindar, though he is sometimes a dandy,
even in the clean and elegantly ornamented streets

and trim gardens of his verse. But he is still a man of cultured taste, delicate though not deep feeling, and some, though not much, poetic force. Mr. Long-fellow has been accused of plagiarism. We have been surprised that any one should have been anx-ious to fasten special charges of this sort upon him, when we had supposed it so obvious that the greater part of his mental stores were derived from the works of others. He has no style of his own growing out of his own experiences and observations of nature. Nature, with him, whether human or external, is always seen through the windows of literature. There are in his poems sweet and tender passages descriptive of his personal feelings, but very few showing him as an observer, at first hand, of the passions within or the landscape without.''

But I will now leave Miss Fuller and Mr. Poe, of whom, I dare say, the readers of this Medley have had more than enough, and introduce them to a pleasanter person than either, the gentleman of whom I have already spoken—Mr. Samuel Ward. That Mr. Ward is an able financier, and a very bright writer, both in prose and verse, is no secret to those who know him or have tracked the streams of his spark-ling fancy along the meadows of light and fugitive literature. The last writing of his that I have seen is a charming paper entitled "Days with Longfellow," in the *North American* for May; and as it bears upon the literary as well as personal history of Mr. Longfellow, I intend to use a page or two of it here. I begin with what he says after mentioning the eminent New-Yorkers who were captivated by the tender grace and the serious purpose of " The Psalm of Life," the popularity of which is as great now as it was forty-five years ago : " I hardly need say that many of the matrons of our city and their young daughters committed the lyrical treasure to memory, and thus formed the nucleus of that expanding circle of English humanity to which so many of Longfellow's future verses became household words. Our correspondence, stimulated, on my part, by admiration for this unsuspected genius of my friend, became and continued for several years extremely active. Sometimes I ventured to suggest a German poem as worthy of being transferred to our language, and, in several cases, a week or a fortnight brought me fresh proof of the marvellous adaptation of his mind and ear to perform what I heard him call, many years after, 'translation, the last infirmity of noble minds.' I was then reading Uhland, and I remember my surprise and delight at his version of the 'Luck of Edenhall' and of the 'Two Locks of Hair,' the latter, I believe, by Gustav Pfizer.

"About this time, during the years from 1838 to 1843, I made a practice of running on to Cambridge to spend Sunday and Monday at the Craigie House, and was always entertained by some new tender or heroic lyric. Once I carried to him Tegnér's 'Children of the Lord's Supper,' which had been given to me by Baron Nordin, then Swedish minister at Washington. Familiar as he was with all the Scandinavian languages, he devoured this poem silently, kept it, and, when I returned a fortnight after, read me his lovely version in the hexameter of the original. It seemed to have been written at one gush, for he took the manuscript from a closet, and I observed that it was written in pencil, with few, if any, corrections. In fact, like the occultists of the East, he seemed noiselessly to have *projected* his work straight from his brain upon the paper. He was a noiseless craftsman, and performed his work with a neatness and despatch I have never seen equalled. He was method itself in all his arrangements, and could lay his hand upon the most minute note or manuscript, however long it had lain hidden in its repository.

"I remember once his writing to me to come on next Sunday, as he had something to show me and to consult me about. I obeyed the call with alacrity, and reached the house, as usual, in season for a tub before breakfast. It was his habit, during the boiling of his coffee-kettle, to work, at a standing-desk, upon a translation of Dante. So soon as the kettle hissed he folded his portfolio, not to resume that work until the following morning. In this wise, by devoting ten minutes a day during many years, the lovely work grew, like a coral reef, to its completion. On the morning of the day in question, however, that task was relinquished, and, after breakfast, he told me that he had recently written a poem which smiled to him, but which his habitual counsellors and companions— who, I presume, were Charles Sumner, C. C. Felton, and George S. Hillard—had frowned upon as beneath the plane of his previous lyrical performances. He then proceeded to read me the ' Skeleton in Armor,' which so stirred my blood that I took the manuscript from his hands and read it to him, with more dramatic force than his modesty had permitted him to display. This may have been presumptuous on my part, but I remember, when I came to the *crescendo*,

> ' As with his wings aslant,
>   Sails the fierce cormorant,
>   Seeking some rocky haunt
>   With his prey laden;
>   So toward the open main,
>   Beating to sea again
>   Through the wild hurricane,
>   Bore I the maiden,'

he sprang to his feet and embraced me. The doubting Thomases were at a discount that morning. This poem revealed to me his methods of work. After the emotions of mutual satisfaction had subsided he told me that he had carried the scheme in his head ever since the previous summer, when, after having visited, with a cavalcade of my brothers and sisters —among whom was the present Mrs. Julia Ward Howe—the skeleton in armor dug up at Taunton, and then visible in a museum at Fall River—since burned to the ground—he challenged my sister, in their home gallop over the Newport beaches, to make a poem out of the rusty hauberk and grim bones they had been inspecting. 'That,' said he, 'was nearly a year ago, and the poem only flashed upon me last week.' It will be remembered that the closing scene is laid

> ' In that tower
> Which to this very hour
> Is looking seaward.'

" And now comes a curious illustration of the market value of poetry, past and present. I proposed to take the manuscript to New York and sell it for not less than fifty dollars. On my return thither my first visit was to the poet Halleck, at his desk in the dingy counting-house of the primeval John Jacob Astor, in

Prince Street. We had often talked about Longfellow, and Halleck felt and displayed a lively appreciation of his genius, which he denied to the English
laureate, whom we all venerate. The old poet was
delighted with this new effusion of his younger lyrical brother, and, knowing the value of his opinion in
the eyes of our literati, I asked him to express his
admiration in a few brief words at the foot of the
manuscript. If I remember rightly the inscription
ran : ' I unhesitatingly pronounce the above to be,
in my opinion, Professor Longfellow's finest effort.'
This was duly signed, and I rushed down to Lewis
Gaylord Clarke, of the *Knickerbocker Magazine*,
who stood aghast when I announced the price of this
poem, he having only paid twenty-five dollars for
its predecessors. The intrinsic beauty of the lyric,
which by this time I had learned to read with tolerable effect, overcame a reluctance to which his poverty, not his will, consented, and I had pride and
pleasure in remitting the fifty dollars to Cambridge
that evening."

Mr. Longfellow's character as a poet was determined by his next volume, " Ballads and Other Poems,"
which was more mature and more robust than
"Voices of the Night," and which made his readers
feel sure that he felt sure of himself. " The Skeleton in Armor" was the most vigorous poem that he

had yet written—a strong conception embodied in terse, picturesque, sweeping words, and in a measure which had not been used, so far as I remember, for more than two centuries—the magnificent measure of old Michael Drayton's "Ballad of Agincourt." I do not see where a line, a phrase even, could be spared or improved. It is as compact, as imperishable, as adamant. Two new elements not previously noticed cropped out in this collection of Mr. Longfellow's song. One was the power of beautifying common things, the clothing of the palpable and familiar with golden, exhalations of the dawn; the other was the oft-renewed and always dangerous experiment of hexameter verse. What I mean by beautifying common things is the making a village blacksmith a subject, and an appropriate subject, for poetry. Mr. Longfellow has done this, I do not know how, and has, likewise, drawn a lesson, for which I care nothing. More purely poetical, more gracious and spiritual, than this paradoxical "Village Blacksmith" are "Endymion" and "Maidenhood," the spirit of the last being as refined as the budding nature which it describes with such exquisite purity and tenderness. Very different from these are "It is not always May," "The Rainy Day," and "God's Acre," each perfect of its kind, and, until one has mastered the art of each kind, of difficult accomplishment. "The

Rainy Day," for example, is in the manner of "The Beleaguered City"—a bad manner, which for once has produced a good poem. "To the River Charles" is a glimpse of Professor Longfellow's early Cambridge life, and the art of it is perfect. By far the most popular piece here, "Excelsior," has more moral than poetical value. The conception of a young man carrying a banner up a mountain suggests a set scene in a drama or opera, and the end of this imaginary stripling does not affect us as it should—does not affect me at all—his attempt to excel being so foolhardy. That he would—that he must—be frozen to death was a foregone conclusion.

The most important of all the translations in Mr. Longfellow's second collection was "The Children of the Lord's Supper," from the Swedish of Tegnér. It revived, as I have intimated, the attempt to naturalize the hexameter in English verse—an attempt which he had made four years before in his paper on "Frithiof's Saga," where he translated into this measure the description of Frithiof's ancestral estate at Framnäs. As I have something to say about the hexameter and its vicissitudes, I must carry my readers back for a moment to the latter half of the sixteenth century, when the poetic mind of Elizabeth's England was clamoring for a new departure in measure. It originated simultaneously, or nearly so, in

the half-addled brains of a number of pedantic poetasters, among whom was Gabriel Harvey, who projected what was called the "English reformed versifying," and what, if it had been successful, would
have reformed versifying out of England, and caused
"a general surceasing of rhyme." This project was
taken up by a coterie who were for abolishing rhyme
altogether and introducing in its stead the Latin sys-
tem of quantity. They amused themselves, and probably bored each other, by writing hexameters, pentameters, sapphics, and what not, and Spenser, who
was drawn into the foolish scheme, worked away for
a twelvemonth (as Professor Child tells us) at hexameters and iambic trimeters quite seriously, going so
far as to write an "Epithalamion Thamesis" in quan-
titative metre, which, happily for his reputation, never
saw the light. One of the first to take this infection
was Master Abraham Fraunce, concerning whom and
his performances Mr. Edward Phillips, in his "Thea-
trum Poetarum" (1675); Mr. William Winstanley,
in "The Lives of the Most Famous English Poets"
(1687); and Mr. Gerard Langbaine, in "An Account of
the English Dramatick Poets" (1691), free their critical minds according to the crabbed fashion of their
period. Mister Ritson—as he insisted upon desig-
nating himself—enumerates, in his "Bibliographia
Poetica," six of Master Fraunce's titles between 1588

and 1592, one being "The Lamentations of Amintas
for the Death of Phillis" ; another, "The Countess of
Pembroke's Emanuel" ; and a third, "Lawyer's Logic" ! It shook—this folly—the fealty to rhyme
of Spenser, Sidney, Dyer, and other lesser lumina-
ries in the heaven of English song. It did not shake
the fealty of Thomas Nash, a savage young satirist,
who immediately declared war upon Harvey, a rope-
maker's son, and upon the hexameter, whom he admitted to be a gentleman of an ancient house (dating
back, he might have added, to the ringing plains of
windy Troy), but who, he conceived, was not at home
in the English language, which was too craggy for
him to run his long plough in—a censure in which
he was anticipated by good old Roger Ascham, who
declared (in substance) that the just-mentioned long
plough trotted and hobbled rather than ran smoothly
therein. After this time and this squabble the un-
fortunate hexameter

"Sank like the day-star in the ocean's bed "

for about two and a quarter centuries, when he
popped up his head again in Southey's "Vision of
Judgment"—a piece of obsequious profanity—and
brought down the bludgeon of Byron upon the heads
of poor Southey and George the Fourth. Such, so
far as I remember, is the history of this alien mea-

sure in English poetry.   Mr. Longfellow thought
well of it, as we have seen, and was justified in so
thinking from the excellence of his own practice in
hexameters.   "The Children of the Lord's Supper"
is a charming poem, to which its antique setting is
very becoming.

Professor Longfellow made a third voyage to Europe shortly after publishing his "Ballads and Other
Poems," and spent the summer months on the Rhine.
The fruits of this leisure were several poems, written
at sea, and expressing his detestation of the Peculiar Institution.   "Poems on Slavery" appeared in
1842, and were dedicated to William Ellery Channing, who did not live to read the poem in which his
character and life-work were commemorated.   The
dedication, which has the ring of Campbell's lyrics
contains a noble stanza :

> " Well done !   Thy words are great and bold;
>   At times they seem to me
>   Like Luther's, in the days of old,
>   Half battles for the free."

"The Slave's Dream" is one of the few remember-
able poems in this volume.   It is exceedingly picturesque, and the movement of the stanzas is spirited and rapid.   If it reminds me of anything it is of
Pringle's "Afar in the Desert," which, however, is

very different, and much more carelessly written.
Even Poe admired "The Slave's Dream," particularly, I believe, the third of the stanzas which follow :

> " Wide through the landscape of his dreams
>   The lordly Niger flowed;
> Beneath the palm-trees on the plain
>   Once more a king he strode;
> And heard the tinkling caravans
>   Descend the mountain-road.
>
> " He saw once more his dark-eyed queen
>   Among her children stand;
> They clasped his neck, they kissed his cheeks,
>   They held him by the hand!—
> A tear burst from the sleeper's lids
>   And fell into the sand.
>
> " And then at furious speed he rode
>   Along the Niger's bank;
> His bridle-reins were golden chains,
>   And, with a martial clank,
> At each leap he could feel his scabbard of steel
>   Smiting his stallion's flank.
>
> " Before him, like a blood-red flag,
>   The bright flamingoes flew;
> From morn till night he followed their flight,
>   O'er plains where the tamarind grew,
> Till he saw the roofs of Caffre huts,
>   And the ocean rose to view.

" At night he heard the lion roar,
    And the hyena scream,
  And the river-horse, as he crushed the reeds
    Beside some hidden stream;
  And it passed, like a glorious roll of drums,
    Through the triumph of his dream."

The fertility of Mr. Longfellow's mind and the variety of his powers were manifested in his thirty-sixth year, in his dramatic study, "The Spanish Student," which was originally published in *Graham's Magazine*, then edited, I believe, by Dr. Griswold, in whose possession I remember to have seen it about thirty years ago. The personages in "The Spanish Student" were the dusky antipodes of the swarthy figures which preceded them. If we judge—and we ought to—this curious production by the intention of its creator and the laws of its construction, it is beautiful. It should be read without the least thought of the stage, which may have been, but should not have been, before the mental eye of the author when he wrote it; and, so read, it will be found radiant with poetry. Not of a passionate or profound kind—which it is not and should not be, for the plot is in no sense a tragic one—but of a kind that suggests the higher walks of serious poetic comedy. The *dramatis personæ* are sketched with sufficient distinctness—as distinctly, it seems to me,

as those in the early comedies of Shakespeare—and
the conversation, which is as lively and bustling as
that of Biron and Rosaline, is suited to the speakers
and their station in Spanish life. The dancing-girl,
Preciosa, is a lovely creation of the poet's fancy.
The sweetest passage in "The Spanish Student,"
which is in praise of woman, is put into the
mouth of the lover of this same dancing-girl, Victorian :

> " What I most prize in woman
>   Is her affections, not her intellect!
>   The intellect is finite; but the affections
>   Are infinite, and cannot be exhausted.
>   Compare me with the great men of the earth;
>   What am I? Why, a pigmy among giants!
>   But if thou lovest—mark me! I say lovest,
>   The greatest of thy sex excels thee not!
>   The world of the affections is thy world,
>   Not that of man's ambition. In that stillness
>   Which most becomes a woman, calm and holy,
>   Thou sittest by the fireside of the heart,
>   Feeding its flame. The element of fire
>   Is pure. It cannot change nor hide its nature,
>   But burns as brightly in a gipsy,camp
>   As in a palace hall. Art thou convinced ? "

Another tender passage drops from the lips of the
same amorist :

" I will forget her!   All dear recollections
Pressed in my heart, like flowers within a book,
Shall be torn out and scattered to the winds!
I will forget her!   But perhaps hereafter,
When she shall learn how heartless is the world,
A voice within her will repeat my name,
And she will say, 'He was indeed my friend!'
Oh! would I were a soldier, not a scholar,
That the loud march, the deafening beat of drums,
The shattering blast of the brass-throated trumpet,
The din of arms, the onslaught and the storm,
And a swift death, might make me deaf for ever
To the upbraidings of this foolish heart!"

The soul of Music breathes out its impassioned
sweetness in the first Act :

SERENADE.

Stars of the summer night!
   Far in yon azure deeps,
Hide, hide your golden light!
   She sleeps!
My lady sleeps!
   Sleeps!

Moon of the summer night!
   Far down yon western steeps,
Sink, sink in silver light!
   She sleeps!
My lady sleeps!
   Sleeps!

> Wind of the summer night!
>   Where yonder woodbine creeps,
> Fold, fold thy pinions light!
>   She sleeps!
> My lady sleeps!
>   Sleeps!
>
> Dreams of the summer night!
>   Tell her her lover keeps
> Watch! while in slumbers light
>   She sleeps!
> My lady sleeps!
>   Sleeps!

Of course Mr. Poe did not like "The Spanish Student." How could he? "Its thesis is unoriginal, its incidents are antique, its plot is no plot, its characters have no character—in short, it is little better than a play upon words to style it 'A Play' at all." Besides, it was pilfered—not so much from the Exemplary Novels of Cervantes as from his own tragicomedy, "Politian":

> "His body is in Segovia,
>   His soul is in Madrid."

Two years after the appearance of this feeble shadow of "Romeo and Juliet" we had bodies of corporeal substance in "The Belfry of Bruges and Other Poems." Traces of Professor Longfellow's early manner as unsuccessfully put forth in "The

Beleaguered City" were triumphant in the prologue, "Carillon," and in "The Arrow and the Song," winged, far-flying, and, as many think, the most perfect of all his smaller pieces.

THE ARROW AND THE SONG.

I shot an arrow into the air,
It fell to earth, I knew not where;
For, so swiftly it flew, the sight
Could not follow it in its flight.

I breathed a song into the air,
It fell to earth, I knew not where;
For who has sight so keen and strong
That it can follow the flight of song?

Long, long afterward in an oak
I found the arrow, still unbroke;
And the song, from beginning to end,
I found again in the heart of a friend.

In the address "To a Child" and in "The Occultation of Orion" Mr. Longfellow reached a table-land of imagination not before attained by his Muse. "The Bridge" is a manifestation of his personality, and of one phase of his genius that has never ceased to charm the great body of his readers, whom it supports upon the broad bosom of the shining Charles, as it supported aforetime the heavy figure of Andrew Craigie, apothecary, and as it supported until

lately the lithe and light figure of Henry Wadsworth
Longfellow.   Hear him as he muses aloud :

" How often, oh! how often,
    In the days that had gone by,
  I had stood on that bridge at midnight,
    And gazed on that wave and sky!

" How often, oh! how often,
    I had wished that the ebbing tide
  Would bear me away on its bosom
    O'er the ocean wild and wide.

" For my heart was hot and restless,
    And my life was full of care,
  And the burden laid upon me
    Seemed greater than I could bear.

" But now it has fallen from me,
    It is buried in the sea;
  And only the sorrow of others
    Throws its shadow over me.

" Yet whenever I cross the river
    On its bridge with wooden piers,
  Like the odor of brine from the ocean
    Comes the thought of other years.

" And I think how many thousands
    Of care-encumbered men,
  Each bearing his burden of sorrow,
    Have crossed the bridge since then.

" I see the long procession
    Still passing to and fro,
 The young heart hot and restless,
    And the old subdued and slow!

" And for ever and for ever,
    As long as the river flows,
 As long as the heart has passions,
    As long as life has woes;

" The moon and its broken reflection
    And its shadows shall appear,
 As the symbol of love in heaven,
    And its wavering image here."

If the train of thought which has been suggested
here is not new, it is because no train of thought that
embraces mankind ever is new. It is tender, pathetic, natural, and that is enough. The lines to "The
Driving Cloud" were Mr. Longfellow's first valuable
contribution to our scanty store of aboriginal poetry
—the forerunner of an immortal production not yet
transmuted into limpid melody. Under the head of
" Songs" came eight poems, two of which were
moulded after a fashion that Mr. Longfellow had
now succeeded in making his own. I refer to "Sea-
Weed" and "The Arrow and the Song"—fantasies
wherethrough the doctrine of poetic correspondences
works out happily and victoriously its own excuse for
being. "The Belfry of Bruges" is a picturesque de-

scription of that quaint old city as beheld from the
tower of the belfry in the market-place one morning
in summer, accompanied by an imaginative remembrance of its past history, which passes before the
kindling eye of the poet like a court masque or
pageant.   Everything is clearly conceived and in
orderly succession, and in no poem that he had yet
written was the hand of the artist so firm.   "Nuremberg," a companion-piece in the same measure, is
distinguished by the same precision of touch and the
same broad excellence.   There is an indescribable
charm, a grace allied to melancholy, in "A Gleam of
Sunshine," which is one of the few poems that refuse
to be forgotten.   "The Arsenal at Springfield" is
didactic, but I cannot perceive how it could be otherwise than didactic and be a poem at all.   A poet
should be a poet first, but he should also be a man,
and a man who concerns himself with the joys and
sorrows of his fellow-creatures.   There was a great
lesson in the burnished arms at Springfield, and a
lesser poet than the Master of Craigie House would
either not have guessed it, or would have missed it :

> " Were half the power that fills the world with terror,
>   Were half the wealth bestowed on camps and courts,
>   Given to redeem the human mind from error,
>   There were no need of arsenals or forts :

" The warrior's name would be a name abhorrèd!
 And every nation that should lift again
Its hand against a brother, on its forehead
 Would wear for evermore the curse of Cain!

" Down the dark future, through long generations,
 The echoing sounds grow fainter and then cease;
And like a bell, with solemn, sweet vibrations,
 I hear once more the voice of Christ say, ' Peace!'

" Peace! and no longer from its brazen portals
 The blast of War's great organ shakes the skies!
But beautiful as songs of the immortals
 The holy melodies of love arise."

Nothing could be more unlike than " The Norman Baron," a study of the mediæval age, and " Rain in Summer," a fresh, off-hand description of a summer shower at Cambridge. My feeling about the last is that it would have been better if it had been cast in a regular stanza instead of its present form, which strikes me as being a singular one, and that it is not improved by the introduction, at the close, of a higher element than that of simple description. The last three sections are poetical and imaginative, but they disturb, it seems to me, the harmony and unity of the poem.

Not many English-writing poets, good fathers as most of them were and are, have addressed poems to their children. Rare old Ben Jonson wrote twelve

mournful lines about his first daughter, Mary, who
died in infancy :

> " At six months' end she parted hence,
>   With safety of her innocence." '

Shakespeare bewailed in " King John " the loss of
his little son Hamnet. Coleridge sang a touching
cradle-song over his poor boy Hartley in " Frost at
Midnight "; Shelley wept bitter tears at the death
of his son William ; Barry Cornwall celebrated the
birth of his lovely daughter Adelaide in a delightful sonnet ; and Leigh Hunt, most melodious of all,
rollicked about two of his children in two characteristic ditties, the most natural of which he inscribed
to his son John in "A Nursery Song for a Four-Year-
Old Romp." These are some of the best-known English poets who have been inspired by children. Professor Longfellow distanced all but Shakespeare, and
apparently without an effort, in his lines "To my
Child." We have in it the first glimpse of the poet's
house, and of the Washington chamber in which
he wrote so many of his poems, and which had now
become his daughter's nursery :

> " With what a look of proud command
>   Thou shakest in thy little hand
>   The coral rattle with its silver bells,
>   Making a merry tune !

Thousands of years in Indian seas
That coral grew, by slow degrees,
Until some deadly and wild monsoon
Dashed it on Coromandel's sand !
Those silver bells
Reposed of yore,
As shapeless ore,
Far down in the deep-sunken wells
Of darksome mines,
In some obscure and sunless place,
Beneath huge Chimborazo's base,
Or Potosí's o'erhanging pines !
And thus for thee, O little child,
Through many a danger and escape,
The tall ships passed the stormy cape ;
For thee in foreign lands remote,
Beneath a burning, tropic clime,
The Indian peasant, chasing the wild goat,
Himself as swift and wild,
In falling, clutched the frail arbute,
The fibres of whose shallow root,
Uplifted from the soil, betrayed
The silver veins beneath it laid,
The buried treasures of the miser, Time."

He turns from the child to the memory of the great
Man whose feet once trod so heavily where hers glide
so lightly :

" Through these once solitary halls
    Thy pattering footstep falls.

The sound of thy merry voice
Makes the old walls
Jubilant, and they rejoice
With the joy of thy young heart,
O'er the light of whose gladness
No shadows of sadness
From the sombre background of memory start.

" Once, ah! once, within these walls,
One whom memory oft recalls,
The Father of his Country, dwelt.
And yonder meadows broad and damp
The fires of the besieging camp
Encircled with a burning belt.
Up and down these echoing stairs,
Heavy with the weight of cares,
Sounded his majestic tread ;
Yes, within this very room
Sat he in those hours of gloom,
Weary both in heart and head.
But what are these grave thoughts to thee ?
Out, out! into the open air:
Thy only dream is liberty,
Thou carest little how or where.
I see thee eager at thy play,
Now shouting to the apples on the tree,
With cheeks as round and red as they ;
And now among the yellow stalks,
Among the flowering shrubs and plants,
As restless as the bee.

Along the garden walks
The tracks of thy small carriage-wheels I trace ;
And see at every turn how they efface
Whole villages of sand-roofed tents,
That rise like golden domes
Above the cavernous and secret homes
Of wandering and nomadic tribes of ants.
Ah! cruel little Tamerlane,
Who, with thy dreadful reign,
Dost persecute and overwhelm
These hapless Troglodytes of thy realm !

" What! tired already! with those suppliant looks,
And voice more beautiful than a poet's books,
Or murmuring sound of water as it flows,
Thou comest back to parley with repose !
This rustic seat in the old apple-tree,
With its o'erhanging golden canopy
Of leaves illuminate with autumnal hues,
And shining with the argent light of dews,
Shall for a season be our place of rest.
Beneath us, like an oriole's pendent nest,
From which the laughing birds have taken wing,
By thee abandoned, hangs thy vacant swing.
Dream-like the waters of the river gleam ;
A sailless vessel drops adown the stream,
And like it, to a sea as wide and deep,
Thou driftest gently down the tides of sleep.

" O child! O new-born denizen
Of life's great city! on thy head

The glory of the morn is shed,
Like a celestial benison!
Here at the portal thou dost stand,
And with thy little hand
Thou openest the mysterious gate
Into the future's undiscovered land.
I see its valves expand,
As at the touch of Fate!
Into those realms of love and hate,
Into that darkness blank and drear,
By some prophetic feeling taught,
I launch the bold, adventurous thought,
Freighted with hope and fear;
As upon subterranean streams,
In caverns unexplored and dark,
Men sometimes launch a fragile bark,
Laden with flickering fire,
And watch its swift-receding beams,
Until at length they disappear,
And in the distant dark expire.

" By what astrology of fear or hope
Dare I to cast thy horoscope!
Like the new moon thy life appears;
A little strip of silver light,
And widening outward into night
The shadowy disk of future years;
And yet upon its outer rim
A luminous circle, faint and dim,
And scarcely visible to us here,
Rounds and completes the perfect sphere;

A prophecy and intimation,
A pale and feeble adumbration,
Of the great world of light that lies
Behind all human destinies.

" Ah! if thy fate, with anguish fraught,
Should be to wet the dusty soil
With the hot tears and sweat of toil,
To struggle with imperious thought
Until the overburdened brain,
Weary with labor, faint with pain,
Like a jarred pendulum, retain
Only its motion, not its power—
Remember, in that perilous hour,
When most afflicted and oppressed,
From labor there shall come forth rest."

"The Day is Done" belongs to a class of poems that depend for their success upon the human element which they suggest or contain, and to which they appeal. "The Old Clock on the Stairs" is an illustration of what I would convey, and as good a one as any with which I am acquainted in the writings of contemporary poets. The humanities, never· long absent from Craigie House, were present in the ticking of the old clock on the stairs, and were chanting a lusty stave as they turned the yellow leaves of the old Danish song-book. What is it that they are trolling out in the haunted shadows of the poet's library ?

"Thou art stained with wine
Scattered from hilarious goblets,
As the leaves with the libations
Of Olympus.

"Yet dost thou recall
Days departed, half forgotten,
When in dreamy youth I wandered
By the Baltic,

"When I paused to hear
The old ballad of King Christian
Shouted from suburban taverns
In the twilight.

"Thou recallest bards
Who, in solitary chambers,
And with hearts by passion wasted,
Wrote thy pages.

"Thou recallest homes
Where thy songs of love and friendship
Made the gloomy Northern winter
Bright as summer.

"Once some ancient Scald,
In his bleak, ancestral Iceland,
Chanted staves of these old ballads
To the Vikings.

"Once in Elsinore,
At the court of old King Hamlet,
Yorick and his boon companions
Sang these ditties.

"Once Prince Frederick's Guard
  Sang them in their smoky barracks:—
  Suddenly the English cannon
  Joined the chorus.

"Peasants in the field,
  Sailors on the roaring ocean,
  Students, tradesmen, pale mechanics,
  All have sung them.

"Thou hast been their friend;
  They, alas! have left thee friendless!
  Yet at least by one warm fireside
  Art thou welcome.

"And, as swallows build
  In these wide, old-fashioned chimneys,
  So thy twittering songs shall nestle
  In my bosom—

"Quiet, close, and warm,
  Sheltered from all molestation,
  And recalling by their voices
  Youth and travel."

This volume introduced Mr. Longfellow in a spe-
cies of composition in which we had not hitherto
seen him, save in translations—the sonnet, of which
there were three specimens here, the best, perhaps,
being on "Dante." One feature of his poetry, and
not the strongest, was the first which his imitators

seized on, and sought to transfer to their own rhymes.
I allude to his habit of comparing one thing with another thing—an outward fact with an inward experience, or *vice versa*.   A few examples will illustrate
what I mean :

> "Before him, like a blood-red flag,
>   The bright flamingoes flew."

> "And it passed like a glorious roll of drums
>   Through the triumph of his dream."

> "Through the closed blinds the golden sun
>   Poured in a dusky beam,
>   Like the celestial ladder seen
>   By Jacob in his dream."

> "And the night shall be filled with music,
>   And the cares that infest the day
>   Shall fold their tents like the Arabs,
>   And as silently steal away."

It was Mr. Longfellow's fancy, not his imagination,
which commended his verse to poetasters of both
sexes throughout the world of English readers, and
what was excellent in him—and is excellent in itself,
when restrained within due bounds—became absurd
in them, it was carried to such excesses.   Mr. Thomas
Buchanan Read was prodigal of comparisons.   A de-

serted road, for instance, sweeps in his verse towards the crowded market,

> ' Like a stream without a sail."

He muses beside this wonderful old road until he opines that he

> " Sees the years descend and vanish
> Like the tented wains and teams."

He is singing about a summer shower, and, with a certain sort of picturesqueness which is marred by incongruous fancies, he sees the silvery rain, in the first stanza,

> " Like a long line of spears, brightly burnished and tall."

In the second stanza it is "like cavalry fleet," and the wild birds listening to the raindrops are "like a musical school," while the rain breaks the face of the spring "like pebbles." Another example, and I have done with Mr. Read's minstrelsy :

> " The shadow of the midnight hours
> Falls like a mantle round my form;
> And all the stars, like autumn flowers,
> Are banished by the whirling storm."

All our minor singers imitated Mr. Longfellow, as the minor singers of an earlier period imitated Mr.

Bryant, and the result was a curious medley of crude thought and far-fetched imagery. It was the experience of Mr. Tennyson anticipated, as he has told us in "The Flower":

> " Read my little fable :
> He that runs may read.
> Most can raise the flowers now,
> For all have got the seed."

Mr. Longfellow's next venture was the gift of his admiring but careless friend Hawthorne. The circumstance that led to this profuse generosity is stated briefly in the first volume of his "American Note-Books," in a congeries of memoranda written between October 24, 1838, and January 4, 1839. *Voilà :* "H. L. C—— heard from a French-Canadian a story of a young couple in Acadie. On their marriage-day all the men of the village were summoned to assemble in the church to hear a proclamation. When assembled they were all seized and shipped off to be distributed through New England, among them the new bridegroom. His bride set off in search of him, wandered about New England all her lifetime, and at last, when she was old, she found her bridegroom on his death-bed. The shock was so great that it killed her likewise." This forcible deportation of a whole people occurred in 1755, when the French, to the extent of eighteen thousand souls, were seized by the English in the manner stated. History, which excuses so much, has perhaps excused the act, but humanity never can. It is as indefensible as the Inquisition.

"Evangeline" disputed the palm with "The Princess," which was published in the same year, 1847. The two poems are so unlike, so divergent, that no comparison can or should be instituted between them. Each shows its writer at his best as a story-teller, and if the mediæval medley surpasses the modern pastoral in richness of coloring—and I think it does —it is surpassed in turn by the tender interest, the pathetic feeling of its younger rival. Both. poems are curious as betraying the mental habits of their authors—the never-satisfied taste of one, the easily and permanently satisfied taste of the other. A great many lines have been written in and out of "The Princess"—the divine lyrics between the books have all been written in—but "Evangeline" stands to-day, I believe, as it was first printed. The English poet always quarrelled with his work; the American poet never quarrelled with his work, nor with any human being, if he could help it. The tautologies that Poe noted in "The Spanish Student" are still there:

> " Never did I behold thee so *attired*
> And *garmented* in beauty as to-night";

and, worse still, this excess of lucidity :

> " What we need
> **Is the celestial fire to change the fruit**
> *Into transparent crystal, bright and clear !* "

Or, more monstrous still, for a Latinist, the inappropriate adjective of this line in " Sand of the Desert in an Hour-Glass " :

> " Its *unimpeded* sky."

But to return to " Evangeline," which I intended to analyze, but shall not. It is what the critics had been so long demanding and clamoring for—an American poem—and it is narrated with commendable simplicity, and a fluency which is not so commendable. Poetry, as poetry merely, is kept in the background ; the descriptions, even when they appear redundant, are subordinated to the main purpose of the poem, out of which they rise naturally ; the characters, if not clearly drawn, are distinctly indicated, and the landscapes through which they move are perfectly characteristic of the New World. It is the French village of Grand-Pré which we behold ; it is the Colonial Louisiana and the remote West—not the fairy-land which Campbell (who might have known better) imagined for himself when he sat down in his study, with a bottle before him, to compose " Gertrude

of Wyoming"—a non-existent Wyoming, with its
shepherd swains tending their flocks on green declivi-
ties, and skimming the lakes with light canoes, while
lovely maidens danced in brown forests to the music
of the flageolet! (Certes, Tam, the bee was buzzin'
in your bonnet then.) Evangeline, loving, patient,
sorrowful maiden, has taken a permanent place
among the heroines of English song; but whether
the picturesque hexameters in which her story is
told will hereafter rank among the standard measures of the language can only be conjectured. Before I quit this vexed question of the adaptability of
the hexameter to English ears I will copy here the
substance of a review of Merivale's translation of
the "Iliad" into English rhymed verse, which I wrote
for the *World* over twelve years ago. I ran through
the early translators of Homer—Chapman, Ogilby,
Hobbes—and passed lightly over the good and bad
points of Pope, Cowper, Morrice, Wright, Sotheby,
Newman, Lord Derby, Blackie, all of which translations I then believed, from the data before me, had
proved failures. Blank verse and rhyme having
failed, what measure is there left for a translator of
Homer? Newman hit upon one, or, to speak more
reverently of that learned and accomplished man of
letters, reasoned out one which he convinced himself
was the great *To Kalon*. It resembles Chapman's,

except that the lines do not rhyme, and that they end with double-syllabled words. It ought to have the flow of the ballad, one would think, and it ought to have the freedom of blank verse; but it has neither, being, in brief, as uncouth and barbaric as the war-song of a Pacific-islander. Newman's failure brought Matthew Arnold out against him, and brought out Arnold's own idea of the way in which Homer should be translated, and the best—the only—measure in which Homer should be done into English. He gave some of the reasons why Chapman, Pope, Cowper, and Newman did not succeed, and some of the reasons why the coming translator ought to succeed, in hexameters. They are plausible but not convincing, for the reason which scholars like himself cannot or *will* not see—that hexameters are foreign to the spirit of the English language, and are, to all but scholars and students in rhythm, difficult and tiresome reading. They have been tried over and over again, and never with success—never with success enough to make them enjoyable to the mass of readers of English poetry. We ought to like them, perhaps; but we do not, and cannot be made to. At any rate, we have not been made to like them, in spite of Clough's "Bothie of Tober-na-Vuolich," Longfellow's "Evangeline," Kingsley's "Andromeda," and the spirited bits of Homer which Arnold himself has given us.

Not to linger longer, however, on the generalities of criticism, let me pick out a passage or two of Homer as it has been rendered by some of the writers I have named, and as it is rendered by Merivale, the general drift of whose measure recalls that of the old ballads, with variations such as have not been introduced into any English version I am acquainted with, which variations, when not original with Merivale, are apparently derived from his studies of our irregular balladists and metrists.

One of the most famous passages in the "Iliad" is the conclusion of the eighth book—the description of moonlight, and the comparison of the Grecian watch-fires to the stars. I will begin with Pope :

" As when the moon, refulgent lamp of night!
   O'er heaven's clear azure spreads her sacred light,
   When not a breath disturbs the deep serene,
   And not a cloud o'ercasts the solemn scene ;
   Around her throne the vivid planets roll,
   And stars unnumbered gild the glowing pole,
   O'er the dark trees a yellower lustre shed,
   And tip with silver every mountain's head ;
   Then shine the vales, the rocks in prospect rise,
   A flood of glory bursts from all the skies ;
   The conscious swains, rejoicing in the sight,
   Eye the blue vault and bless the useful light.

So many flames before proud Ilion blaze,
And lighten glimmering Xanthus with their rays;
The long reflections of the distant fires
Gleam on the walls and tremble on the spires.
A thousand piles the dusky horrors gild,
And shoot a shady lustre o'er the field.
Full fifty guards each flaming pile attend,
Whose umbered arms, by fits, thick flashes send;
Loud neigh the coursers o'er their heaps of corn,
And ardent warriors wait the rising morn."

This florid and ornate passage was much extolled
by Pope's contemporaries, and justly enough, according to their false poetic standard; but judged by the
higher standard of to-day—higher, that is, in regard
to poetry in general, and the poetry of Homer in particular—it would not be easy to find anything more
radically bad as poetry, and more unfaithful to the
sense and manner of Homer.   Nothing can be worse
than the feeble Latinity of "refulgent lamp of
night," and nothing more prosaic than "rocks in
prospect rise," "conscious swains," "ardent warriors," etc.   There is nothing in Homer about gilding
the pole; nothing about the reflections of the fires
gleaming on walls and trembling on spires; nothing,
in a word, that justifies the mincing elegance of Pope.
What Homer did say in the passage so emasculated
may be got at through Buckley's prose version of the

"Iliad," where its substance remains intact, though lacking, of course, the rich, poetic, old-world atmosphere of the original:

"As when in heaven the stars appear very conspicuous around the lucid moon, when the ether is wont to be without a breeze, and all the pointed rocks and lofty summits and groves appear; but in heaven the immense ether is disclosed, and all the stars are seen, and the shepherd rejoices in his soul. Thus did many fires of the Trojans kindling then appear before Ilium between the ships and the stream of Xanthus. A thousand fires blazed with flame, and by each sat fifty men at the light of the blazing fire. But their steeds, eating white barley and oats, standing by the chariots, awaited beautiful-throned Aurora."

Cowper's version is better than Pope's, but weakened by Latinity, and one or two feeble Miltonic inversions. The last two lines are flat enough:

"As when around the clear bright moon the stars
  Shine in full splendor, and the winds are hushed,
  The groves, the mountain-tops, the headlong heights
  Stand all apparent, not a vapor streaks
  The boundless blue, but ether opened wide
  All glitters, and the shepherd's heart is cheered;
  So numerous seemed those fires the bank between
  Of Xanthus, blazing, and the fleet of Greece,
  In prospect all of Troy—a thousand fires,
  Each watched by fifty warriors seated near.

> The steeds beside the chariots stood, their corn
> Chewing, and waiting till the golden-throned
> Aurora should restore the light of day."

Lord Derby's version is somewhat better, and Newman's not bad—for Newman, though his long lines
are weakened by such phrases as "bursteth" and
"seemeth," and the interpolation "I say." But let
us see how Merivale renders it:

> "As when the stars in heaven burn round their shining
>   queen
> Brilliantly, and without a breath expands the broad serene;
> And every cliff and valley stands out, and headlong height;
> And breaks o'er all the firmament immeasurable light;
> The stars all sparkle, and the swain's heart gladdens at the
>   sight:—
> So many 'twixt the galleys and Xanthus' yellow stream,
> Kindled in front of Ilium, the Trojan bale-fires gleam;
> In the plain bale-fires a thousand are burning, and by each
> In firelight glow full fifty men their limbs reclining stretch;
> And ranged beside their chariots, and munching pulse and
>   corn,
> Their steeds await the fair-pavilioned Goddess of the Morn."

If the old English ballad measure is not the best
one to render Homer in, it is, I think, better than
the heroic couplets of Pope and the blank verse of
Cowper. Its defect, in Merivale's hands, is a ten-
dency to indulge in expansion of his original, and to

make it clearer, or, more strictly speaking, to bring it nearer home to us by allusions to modern customs, as in the instance under consideration, by the use of the word " bale-fires," which is perfectly in keeping in our old ballads, but not quite in keeping in Homer. But let us see what Arnold makes of this passage in hexameters :

" So shone forth, in front of Troy, by the bed of Xanthus,
 Between that and the ships, the Trojans' numerous fires.
 In the plain there were kindled a thousand fires: by each one
 There sat fifty men in the ruddy light of the fires:
 By their chariots stood the steeds, and champed the white barley,
 While their masters sat by the fire, and waited for Morning."

Arnold has written better hexameters than these, as I shall show by and by ; so I will say nothing of those just quoted, but pass on to another version of this passage—the best that I have yet seen. It is by one who possesses many qualities indispensable to the future translator of Homer—Tennyson :

 " As when in heaven the stars about the moon
 Look beautiful, when all the winds are laid,
 And every height comes out, and jutting peak
 And valley, and the immeasurable heavens
 Break open to their highest, and all the stars
 Shine, and the shepherd gladdens in his heart :

> So many a fire between the ships and stream
> Of Xanthus blazed before the towers of Troy,
> A thousand on the plain; and close by each
> Sat fifty in the blaze of burning fire;
> And, champing golden grain, the horses stood
> Hard by their chariots, waiting for the dawn."

Pope nowhere appears to more advantage than in the interview between Hector and Andromache, especially where he describes the child's fright at the helmet of his father. He exercised all his artistic ingenuity in writing the passage below, as may be seen by the fac-simile of a page of it, made from the existing MS. of the rough draft in the British Museum, and to be found in some editions of Disraeli's " Curiosities of Literature " :

> " Thus having spoke, the illustrious chief of Troy
> Stretched his fond arms to clasp the lovely boy.
> The babe clung crying to his nurse's breast,
> Scared at the dazzling helm and nodding crest.
> With secret pleasure each fond parent smiled,
> And Hector hasted to relieve his child :
> The glittering terrors from his brows unbound,
> And placed the beaming helmet on the ground,
> Then kissed the child, and, lifting high in air,
> Thus to the gods preferred a father's prayer."

This is Pope at his best, I think, and very pretty writing it is. Very different is the version of Chapman, whose rough and careless lines remind one of the vigorous sketches of the old masters :

" This said, he reached to take his son; who of his arms afraid,
  And then the horse-hair plume, with which he was so over-
    laid,
  Nodded so horribly, he clinged back to his nurse and cried.
  Laughter affected his great sire, who doffed and laid aside
  His fearful helm, that on the earth cast round about it light;
  Then took and kissed his loving son; and (balancing his
    weight
  In dancing him) these loving vows to living Jove he used,
  And all the other bench of gods. "

As I have quoted nothing yet from Newman, the reader, if unacquainted with his Homer, may like to see what he makes out of this pretty little bit of domestic life, which is as fresh and natural to-day as it was three thousand years ago :

" Thus saying, gallant Hector stretched his arms toward his
    infant;
  But back into the bosom of the nurse with dapper girdle
  The child recoiled with wailing, scared by his dear father's
    aspect,
  In terror dazzled to behold the brass and crest of horse-hair
  Which, from the helmet's topmost ridge, terrific o'er him
    nodded.
  Then did his tender father laugh, and laughed his queenly
    mother,

And gallant Hector instantly beneath his chin the helmet
Unfastened; so upon the ground he laid it, all resplendent,
Then poised his little son aloft, and dandled him and kissed
   him,
And raised a prayer to Jupiter and other gods immortal."

More to my taste than either of these renderings is
Merivale's, which contains a specimen of his variations of the common ballad measure in the short line
sandwiched into his first couplet, which rhymes, as
will be perceived, with the middle of the last line of
the couplet:

" This said, bright-crested Hector reached forth to take his child;
   The infant viewed him with affright,
   And, shrilly screaming at the sight, in his nurse's arms re-
      coiled,
   Scared by the brazen armor, and the helmet's horse-hair
      plume
   Nodding above the lofty crest and waving all its gloom.
   Smiled sire and reverend mother; but Hector from his head
   The helmet loosed, and on the ground the shining trophy laid;
   Then kissed the child and tossed him, and to his bosom pressed,
   And thus almighty Jove in prayer and all the gods addressed."

The passage immediately preceding this, in which
Hector replies to his wife, who has endeavored to
persuade him not to expose his life as he has done,
is pathetically rendered by Merivale, but not near
so finely as by Arnold, who still fails, however, to

make us admire his hexameters, grave and well sustained as we cheerfully admit them to be:

" Woman, I too take thought for this; but then I bethink me
    What the Trojan men and Trojan women might murmur,
    If like a coward I skulked behind, apart from the battle.
    Nor would my own heart let me—my heart, which has bid me
        be valiant
    Always, and always fighting among the first of the Trojans,
    Busy for Priam's fame and my own, in spite of the future.
    For that day will come, my soul is assured of its coming,
    It will come, when sacred Troy shall go to destruction—
    Troy, and warlike Priam too, and the people of Priam.
    And yet not that grief, which then will be, of the Trojans
    Moves me so much—not Hecuba's grief, nor Priam my father's,
    Nor my brethren's, many and brave, who then will be lying
    In the bloody dust under the feet of the foemen—
    As thy grief, when, in tears, some brazen-coated Achaian
    Shall transport thee away, and the day of thy freedom be ended.
    Then, perhaps, thou shalt work at the loom of another, in
        Argos,
    Or bear pails to the well of Messeis, or Hypercia,
    Sorely against thy will, by strong Necessity's order.
    And some man may say, as he looks and sees thy tears falling:
    See, the wife of Hector, that great pre-eminent captain
    Of the horsemen of Troy, in the day they fought for their city.
    So some man will say; and then thy grief will redouble
    At the want of a man like me, to save thee from bondage.
    But let me be dead, and the earth be mounded above me,
    Ere I hear thy cries, and thy captivity told of."

There is a strong flavor of Homer here ; but if Lord
Derby and Merivale interpret the feeling of the
opening line correctly, the phrase "woman" is un-
necessarily harsh. Nor are we satisfied to have
Priam characterized by the epithet "warlike," when
the original makes him "armed with good ashen
spear," which Newman translates "ashen-speared,"
and Merivale "prince of the ashen spear." And
this, by the way, reminds me that Arnold follows
Pope in making the masters of the horses, and not
the horses themselves, watch for the morning. His
reason for the change is ingenious, but overstrained—
as much so, I think, as Ruskin's comment on the
epithet "life-giving," which follows Helen's mention
of her brothers as alive, when they were in reality
dead. "The poet," says Ruskin, "has to speak of
the earth in sadness ; but he will not let that sadness
change his thought of it. No ; though Castor and
Pollux be dead, yet the earth is our mother still—
fruitful, life-giving." "This," Arnold remarks, and
I must apply the censure to him as well as to Ruskin
—"this is just a specimen of that sort of application
of modern sentiment to the ancients against which a
student who wishes to feel the ancients truly cannot
too resolutely defend himself."

The passage just alluded to (it is in the third book
of the "Iliad") has been very nobly translated by Dr.

Hawtrey, late provost of Eton, and, as it is short, I will give it here:

" Clearly the rest I behold of the dark-eyed sons of Achaia;
  Known to me well are the faces of all; their names I remember;
  Two, two only remain, whom I see not among the commanders,
  Kastor, fleet in the car; Polyduktus, brave with the cestus—
  Own dear brethren of mine: one parent loved us as infants.
  Are they not here, in the host, from the shores of loved Lakedaimon,
  Or, though they came with the rest in ships that bound through the waters,
  Dare they not enter the fight or stand in the Council of Heroes,
  All for fear of the shame and the taunts my crime has awakened ?
  So said she—they long since in Earth's soft arms were reposing,
  There, in their own dear land, their fatherland, Lakedaimon."

This is, perhaps, the best specimen of hexameters in the language (it is certainly the best I have ever seen), and I do not say that Homer, so rendered, could not be read with considerable pleasure. But, unfortunately, Homer has *not* been so rendered, and cannot, I am persuaded, be so rendered throughout, for reasons which exist in the very structure of our language, and which will readily suggest themselves to the students thereof. Let me see now what Merivale makes of the passage in his fluent rhymes:

> " ' And all the rest behold I, the Greeks with glancing eyes,
> And well can I remember all their names and histories.
> But two discern I cannot—two princes have I missed:
> Castor, the queller of the steed, and Pollux, stout of fist;
> Two children of one mother, and brothers both to me.
> What! have they not with the others sailed from the land
>   beyond the sea ?
> Or swam they in their galleys from Lacedæmon's shore,
> But now, by keen reproaches stung,
> And hate and scorn upon me flung, join they the fight no
>   more ?'
> So spake she; but those heroes there, on the Spartan
>   strand,
> Already fruitful Earth confined in their dear native land."

From this long digression about what Lord Derby called the "pestilent heresy" of the hexameter I return to "Evangeline," which seemed likely at one time to have a long line of followers, the first of which, "The Bothie of Tober-na-Vuolich," was only a year after it, and the second, "Andromeda," only ten years more. Later experiments of this kind have been made by Mr. E. C. Stedman in his translations from Theocritus, Homer, and Æschylus; by Mr. Bayard Taylor in his "Home Pastorals"; by Mr.

Arthur J. Munby in his "Dorothy" (though that, by the way, is in pentameters) ; and by Mr. Paul Pastnor in "Lora." If I dared to prophesy it would be that the hexameter will never attain such currency in English as it has attained in German in Voss's Homer and in Goethe's "Hermann und Dorothea," which is the forerunner of all similar and later productions in the same school, beginning with "Evangeline" and ending at present with "Dorothy."

What impresses me most strongly while I read Mr. Longfellow is the extent of his poetic sympathy, and the ease with which he passes from one class of subjects to another. His instinct is sure in his choice of all his subjects, and his perception of their poetic capacities never at fault. They translate themselves readily into his language, and he clothes them in their singing-robes when the spirit moves him.

He was a very rapid writer, all things considered ; for, while literature in a certain sense was his profession, the business of his life was to be Professor of Languages and Belles-Letters at Harvard. "Evangeline" was succeeded in 1845 by "The Poets of Europe," a large and scholarly contribution to English literature, of which Mr. Longfellow was the editor, and which contained specimens of European poets in ten different languages, representing the

labors of upwards of one hundred translators, includ-
ing himself. Four years later he published "Kavanagh," which had no plot to speak of, though its
sketches of character were bright and amusing, and
its glimpses of New England life enjoyable. "The
Seaside and the Fireside" came next (1850), then
"The Golden Legend" (1851), and then "The Song
of Hiawatha" (1855), all of which added to his reputation. There are twenty-three poems in "The
Seaside and the Fireside," no two of which are
alike, though all authenticate the cunning hand by
which they were wrought. The most important
poem in the collection is "The Building of the
Ship." I may be singular in my opinion, but
my opinion nevertheless is that "The Building of
the Ship" is a better poem than "The Song of
the Bell." I think its theme is more adapted to
poetic treatment than Schiller's theme—partly, no
doubt, because it is more tangible to the imagination, and capable, therefore, of more definite presen-
tation before the eye of the mind; but largely, I
suppose, because its associations are not attached to
so many memories as cluster about the ringing of a
bell. Its unity is in its self-concentration.

"The Golden Legend" carries us back to the Middle Ages, of which we had transitory gleams in the
earlier writings of Mr. Longfellow. The poetic

atmosphere of that remote period—lovelier to our
Gothic imaginations than the more distant past of
Greece and Rome—envelops a lovely story, which
turns, like the story of "Evangeline," upon the love
and devotion of woman, which here are happily re-
warded. The figure of the peasant girl Elsie, who
determines to sacrifice her life to restore her
prince to the sanity of happiness, is worthy of a
high place in any poet's dream of fair woman—as
high a place as that filled by Joan of Arc,

> " Or her who knew that Love can vanquish Death,
>   Who kneeling, with one arm about her king,
> Drew forth the poison with her balmy breath,
>   Sweet as new buds in Spring."

The charm of the poem, apart from its poetry, is
the thorough and easy scholarship of the poet, who
contrives to conceal the evidences of his reading—an
art which few poets have possessed in an equal degree, which Moore did not possess at all, but which
was masterly in Scott and eminent in Shakespeare.
If the opinion of an unlettered man is worth anything—and it cannot be worth much—the miracle-
play of "The Nativity" is conceived in the very
spirit of those archaic entertainments which cleric
pens devised for the edification of the laity. So far
as I know, it had no prototype in modern English

poetry, and has had no successor worthy of it, except Mr. Swinburne's "Masque of Queen Bersabe." Mr. Ruskin, whose opinions are often sound in spite of the extravagance of his language, detects one phase of the poem in the fourth volume of his "Modern Painters," and states it with unusual brevity: "Longfellow, in 'The Golden Legend,' has entered more closely into the temper of the Monk, for good and evil, than ever yet theological writer or historian, though they may have given their life's labor to the analysis."

Poets are distinguished from writers of verse not only by superiority of genius but by superiority of knowledge. The one has insight, the other outsight merely. The versifier gropes about in search of poetical subjects, while the poet goes to them directly, instinctively, and always finds them, often where others had sought for them in vain. That there was, or might be, a poetic element in the American Indian several ambitious American poets had persuaded themselves, and, so persuaded, had striven to quicken their sluggish numbers with its creative energies. Robert C. Sands and James Wallis Eastburn wrote together the ponderous poem of "Yamoyden"; Charles Fenno Hoffman wrote "A Vigil of Faith"; Seba Smith, a "Powhatan"; Alfred B. Street, a "Frontenac"; and others, I dare say, other aboriginal epics whose names are forgotten. They were unanimous in one thing—they failed to interest their readers. The reason of this was not far to seek and find, we can see, since success has been achieved, but it demanded a vision which was not theirs—the vision and the faculty divine—and which, it seemed, only one American poet had in its fulness. This man saw that the Indian himself, as he moves duskily through our history, was not in himself a poetic hero. But he also saw that he had a poetic side to him, and that if it existed anywhere it existed in his legends. That he had many legends, and that they were remarkably primitive, was well known. They were brought to light by the late Mr. Henry Rowe Schoolcraft, who heard of their existence among the Odjibwa Nation, inhabiting the region about Lake Superior in 1822. Specimens of these unique traditions were published by him in his "Travels in the Central Portions of the Mississippi Valley" (1825) and his "Narrative of the Expedition to Itasca Lake" (1834); but they were not given to the world in their entirety until 1839, in his "Algic Researches." They were as good as manuscript (as the bibliographers say) during the next sixteen years, though one American poet had mastered them thoroughly. This was Mr. Longfellow, who turned this Indian Edda, as he happily calls it, into "The Song of Hiawatha." The immediate

and immense success of this poem, and the increase
of reputation which it hurried upon the writer, recalled the early years of the present century, when
Scott and Byron were sure of thousands of readers,
and thousands of pounds, when it pleased them to
rattle off a metrical romance — a "Lady of the
Lake," a "Marmion," or a "Lara." "The Song of
Hiawatha" was read by all classes, who at once
found themselves interested in the era of flint-
arrow heads, earthen pots, and skin clothes, and its
elemental inhabitants, who, dead centuries before, if
they ever existed, are now living the everlasting life
of Poetry. It passed through many editions in the
United States, in England, and elsewhere in the Old
World in other languages. Its value as a contribution to mythology and ethnology was universally admitted, but the fitness of its form was questioned, as
all new forms are sure to be ; for the form was new to
most readers, though not to scholars in the literatures
of northern Europe. Mr. Longfellow's unscholarly
admirers declared that it was original with him. No,
his enemies answered, he has borrowed it from the
Finnish epic, "The Kalevala." The quarrel, which
was a pretty one while it lasted, was stimulated by
critical paragraphists—who are never happy except
when they are hectoring each other—but nobody else
cared a button about it. The novel singularity of

the body of this Indian Edda led to innumerable parodies, but to nothing serious that I remember, unless Doesticks is to be considered seriously; this circumstance I take to be a silent verdict against its permanency—even against its adoption—in English versification. That the poetry of Professor Longfellow has changed much in the last twenty years I do not perceive, except that it has grown graver and more meditative in its purpose. Its technical excellence has steadily increased, until what was once artifice has become Art. Professor Longfellow has held his own against all English-writing poets, and in no walk of poetry so positively as in that of telling a story. In an age of story-tellers he stands at their head—Master of many scholars—not only in the narrative poems that I have mentioned, but in the lesser stories included in his "Tales of a Wayside Inn," to which the literatures of the whole world have lavishly contributed. He preceded by several years the author of "The Earthly Paradise" and artistic wall-papers, who has no abiding sense of the value of time, and not the shadow of a suspicion that there may be too much of a good thing. I admire Mr. Morris—no one more—but I would rather praise than read his long narratives in verse. Which is but another way of saying that I prefer short poems to long ones. About the only piece of criticism that Poe

ever wrote to which I can assent without qualifica-
tion is, that long poems are mistakes. A poem proper should produce a unity of impression, which can
be obtained only within a reasonable time ; it should
never provoke the reader into closing the book. This
may be destructive criticism, but I am inclined to
think there is something in it, although it is disre-
spectful to the memory of Milton. A Poem should be
read at a single sitting. Any of Shakespeare's great
Tragedies can be read at a single sitting, but " Paradise Lost" cannot. There must go to the reading
of, that grandiose epic as many sittings as there are
books. One suffices for "Comus" or "Samson Ago-
nistes." Any of Professor Longfellow's stories, long
or short, can be read without rising from the chair.
As he had always shown good taste, it was a foregone conclusion that he would delight us with his
"Tales of a Wayside Inn." Every old tale therein was worth a new version, even " The Falcon of Sir
Fedrigo," which young Barry Cornwall pursued
when Master Longfellow was at school. Mr. Longfellow's method of telling a story will compare favor-
ably with the method of any English story-telling
poet from the days of Chaucer. His heroic couplets
are as facile as those of Hunt and Keats, from whose
affectations and mannerisms he is free. They suggest
the heroics of no other poet, American or English,

and, unlike some of his early verses, are without man-
nerism. They as surely attain a pure poetic style as
the prose of Hawthorne attains a pure prose style.

The most distinctive of Mr. Longfellow's poems are
probably those which he entitled "Birds of Passage," and prophetically, for they have flown into
many lands and into all hearts. What first impresses
me in reading them is the multifarious reading of
their writer, who appeared to have no favorite authors, but to read for the delight that he took in reading. He had the art of finding unwritten poems in the
most out-of-the-way books and in even every-day oc-
currences. When the Duke of Wellington died he
hymned his departure in "The Warden of the Cinque
Ports," which the populace preferred to the Laureate's scholarly Ode. His good friend Hawthorne
went before him, and he embalmed his memory and
his unfinished romance in imperishable verse :

> " I only hear above his place of rest
>   Their tender undertone,
>   The infinite longings of a troubled breast,
>   The voice so like his own.

> " There in seclusion and remote from men
>   The wizard hand lies cold,
>   Which at its topmost speed let fall the pen,
>   And left the tale half told.

> " Ah ! who shall lift that wand of magic power,
>   And the lost clew regain?
> The unfinished window in Aladdin's tower
>   Unfinished must remain !"

Charles Sumner died, his dear friend of many long years, and ever his admirer, and he bewailed him as tenderly and sadly as the young Manrique bewailed his father:

> " Were a star quenched on high,
>   For ages would its light,
> Still travelling downward from the sky,
>   Shine on our mortal sight.

> " So, when a great man dies,
>   For years beyond our ken
> The light he leaves behind him lies
>   Upon the paths of men."

I have been looking over a few of Mr. Longfellow's notes to me, and have concluded to insert them here in the order in which they were written, elucidating them where I can:

"Camb., Jan. 8, 1878.

"Dear Mr. Stoddard: Please accept my thanks for your kind letter, for the poems you send me and those you refer to in Griswold.

"I have not his 'Female Poets' at hand, but shall lose no time in getting a copy and examining the poems you mention.

"Your tribute to Lincoln is beautiful and very just. I will keep it carefully out of sight till it appears in the magazine.

"As to your estimate of Mrs. Stoddard's literary abilities, I do not wonder at it. You do not rate them a bit too high; and if her writings have not found that swift recognition which they merit, I hope it will not discourage her. Often the best things win their way slowly, but are pretty sure of being found out sooner or later.

"Some of your volumes I have. The rest I shall find in the libraries, here or in Boston. I thank you for pointing out the pieces that will be of use to me. I have frequently been obliged to omit poems of merit because I could not ascertain their localities.

"I was very glad to renew my acquaintance with you at the pleasant Atlantic Dinner, and am, with great regard,

"Yours very truly,
"HENRY W. LONGFELLOW."

"CAMB., Jan. 14, 1878.

"DEAR MR. STODDARD: The three handsome volumes of Griswold have arrived safely, and I hasten to thank you for your great kindness in sending them. Though I have not yet had time to examine them carefully, yet I have glanced at them here and there, and see that they will be of much use to me.

"I wish I had possessed a copy of the 'Female Poets' sooner. I should not then have missed those three striking poems by Mrs. Stoddard—'The Bull-Fight,' 'El Capitano,' and 'On the Campagna,' whose absence in 'Poems of Places' I much regret.

"With renewed thanks for your careful kindness,

"Yours very truly,
"HENRY W. LONGFELLOW."

"CAMB., April 28, 1878.

"DEAR MR. STODDARD: I am much obliged to you for the 'Earlier Poems' of Mrs. Browning, and for your fine Ode, 'Hospes Civitatis,' which is strong and beautiful.

"I am sorry that it comes to me too late for India; but it is in season for China and the Nile, and I am very glad to have it. Those regions will be the richer for it. Thanks.

"In great haste,
"Yours very truly,
"HENRY W. LONGFELLOW."

The following note refers to a poem which I had the honor of reading before the young gentlemen of Harvard:

"CAMB., June 30, 1878.

"DEAR MR. STODDARD: I was very sorry and much disappointed not to see you and Mrs. Stoddard when you were here last week. But it was such a busy week that I could not go to town in search of you, and probably should not have found you if I had gone.

"I failed also to hear you deliver your poem. Being delayed by visitors, and thinking the poem would follow the oration, I arrived too late.

"The next best thing to hearing the poem is reading it. Thanks for the opportunity of doing so thus early. It is both vigorous and beautiful. The warlike ages you have described with a tumult of verse finely adapted to the theme.

"Fifty years ago, before the same society, Bryant recited his poem, 'The Ages,' in Spenserian stanzas. On the year of his death you take up the theme once more, and paint an Historic Picture in the same metre. Was it accident or design? I know not; but whichever it was, the idea is very felicitous. I congratulate you on your success.

"I was glad to see Mr. Gifford. He made some capital sketches, with which I think you will be pleased.

"Yours very truly,

"HENRY W. LONGFELLOW."

"CAMB., Sept. 8, 1878.

"DEAR MR. STODDARD: Your sketch is more than satisfactory, and the frank and easy style in which it is written adds to its attraction.

"I return it to the editor to-day, with one or two corrections in the genealogy, etc.

" Please correct also what you say of translations of Homer in hexameters. I have two : one by Herschel, 1866, and another by Cochrane, 1867. Whether these preceded or followed Arnold's suggestion I cannot say, as I have not his book at hand.

" Please tell me by postal-card where Harley River is. I wish to have it in ' Poems of Places,' but do not find it in the Gazetteer.

" Yours, with many thanks,
" HENRY W. LONGFELLOW.

" P.S.—One omission I notice. You say nothing of my translation of the 'Divina Commedia,' published in 1867, which perhaps it would be well to notice, if only to correct an error in regard to its composition.

" In the ' Life and Letters of Ticknor ' (ii. 479) it is stated that I was engaged upon it ' over five-and-twenty years.'

" In Mr. Richardson's ' Primer of American Literature,' p. 55, the time is magnified into ' more than thirty years.'

" The fact is, I was engaged upon it, as I find by dates in the MS., just two years (Feb. 20, 1862–Feb. 4, 1864)."

I have omitted one note from its proper place, but I shall publish it after the following hasty review of Mr. Longfellow's " Keramos " in the *Independent* of May 16, 1878, to which it refers, and which I had entirely forgotten :

"About the beginning of the present century a German poet, who had written well in many directions, reached the great audience of his countrymen by a song—if it may be called such—which has been popular ever since and in all lands. I allude to Schiller and his 'Song of the Bell,' which has been the model that other poets have kept before them when writing upon similar themes. Mr. Longfellow, for example, followed the shining trail of that divine singer of labor in 'The Building of the Ship'—a beautiful craft which was launched upon the wide sea of literature twenty-eight years ago.

"Mr. Thomas Buchanan Read, who began his career as an imitator of Mr. Longfellow and ended as an imitator of everybody, struck a more earthly key in 'The Brickmaker'; and Mr. Samuel Ferguson, an Irish poet, smote a lusty lyric in his 'Forging of the Anchor.' Akin to these productions was 'The Bells' of Poe, the sound of whose verse in that marvellous epical ditty echoes and re-echoes the sense, and conveys the exact impression that he intended.

"There must be something very attractive in this class of subjects, or so practical a poet and so clear a thinker as Mr. Longfellow would not have returned to it, as he has just done in 'Keramos and Other Poems.' He has excelled himself in the poem which gives this volume its name, and, if any of the English versions of 'The Song of the Bell' do it justice (which is scarcely probable), he has at least equalled Schiller. 'Keramos' is a series of artistic conceptions, which are thoroughly and perfectly executed.

The work of the potter grows under his shaping hands, while he sings a refrain which perpetually changes and deepens, and which exhausts the inner meaning of his handiwork:

> "'Where more is meant than meets the ear.'

"The poet is borne along on the wings of his singing until he reaches and passes the world's great pottery places—Delft, Saintes (where he sees Palissy burning his furniture to keep his furnace going), and the studios of Gubbio, Xanto, Georgio, and Lucca della Robbia. The treasures of Etruria are restored:

> " ' Vases and urns, and bas-reliefs,
> Memorials of forgotten griefs,
> Or records of heroic deeds—
> Of demigods and mighty chiefs.'

The swift wings of his genius transport him (the potter working and singing meanwhile) to Egypt, where he has on either bank of the Nile huge water-wheels,

> " ' Belted with jars and dripping weeds,'

and where he has visions of the old Egyptian deities —Ammon, Osiris, and Isis—crowned and veiled.

> " ' The sacred Ibis, and the Sphinx;
> Bracelets with blue enamelled links;
> The Scarabee in emerald mailed,
> Or spreading wide his funeral wings;

> Lamps that perchance their night-watch kept
> O'er Cleopatra while she slept—
> All plundered from the tombs of kings.'

Bird-like he flies over the Ganges and over the Himalayas to the Central Flowery Kingdom, where he hovers over the town of King-te-tching, where three thousand furnaces are burning—a great grove of chimneys, which whirls its leaves of porcelain to all the markets of the world. He sees things beautiful (as those almond-eyed artists understand beauty) and things useful:

> " ' The willow pattern, that we knew
> In childhood, with its bridge of blue
> Leading to unknown thoroughfares;
> The solitary man who stares
> At the white river flowing through
> Its arches, the fantastic trees
> And wild perspective of the view.'

He sees the Tower of Porcelain, and the grandeur and beauty of the landscapes of Japan, which are so fantastically reproduced in its pottery-work. Picture after picture passes before his eyes and before ours—thanks to his beautiful gift of poetry—in a succession of exquisite melodies, which flow on and along to a music of their own making.

"The second section of the volume, 'Birds of Passage,' opens with 'The Herons of Elmwood,' which everybody knows is the residence of the poet Lowell, a stately old mansion haunted with scholarly memories. The herons are called upon to sing of the

air, of the wild delight of the wings that uphold
them, the rapture of flight through the mists that
enfold them, of the landscapes below and the splendor of light above, and are told to ask the poet if the
songs of the Troubadours and Minnesingers are sweeter than theirs :

"'And if yours are sweeter and wilder and better.'

Say to him at his gate that some one hath lingered
there and sends him a friendly greeting :

"' That many another hath done the same,
    Though not by a sound was the silence broken;
    The surest pledge of a deathless name
    Is the silent homage of thoughts unspoken.'

"This charming poem refutes the notion that there
is no genuine friendship and intellectual recognition
among poets.   Mr. Longfellow has always been ready
to stretch forth the hand of good-fellowship toward
his fellow-singers, and no previous volume of his
shows such a readiness as the one before us, which
contains, in addition to this poem, a sonnet addressed to Tennyson, wherein his mastery is proclaimed.
We must quote its terzettes, which are admirable :

"' Not of the howling dervishes of song,
    Who craze the brain with their delirious dance,
    Art thou, O sweet historian of the heart !
    Therefore to thee the laurel-leaves belong,
    To thee our love and our allegiance,
    For thy allegiance to the poet's art.'

Could anything be more characteristic of the present

school of spasmodic poetry than that phrase 'howling dervishes'? Another proof of the friendship of men of genius is the sonnet entitled 'The Three Silences' (which are those of speech, desire, and thought), addressed to the poet Whittier. We can recall no tribute to the Quaker singer which is at once so just and so discriminating as the conclusion of this noble sonnet :

> " ' O thou, whose daily life anticipates
> The life to come, and in whose thought and word
> The spiritual world preponderates,
> Hermit of Amesbury ! thou too hast heard
> Voices and melodies from beyond the gates,
> And speakest only when thy soul is stirred.'

"'There are sixteen 'Birds of Passage' here, and they have flown from many lands. 'A Dutch Picture' tells the story of its nativity in its title, which, however, gives no hint of the Flemish landscapes and gardens and interiors that are painted therein. It is thoroughly in keeping and admirable as a gallery of figure-pieces. 'Castles in Spain' is still more picturesque and delightful, exhausting, as it does, a world of historic, personal, and architectural associations, completing the circle of Spanish poetry which Mr. Longfellow began with his 'Coplas de Manrique,' continued in 'The Spanish Student,' and has closed in this felicitous production. From Spain he passes to Italy in 'Vittoria Colonna,' a melodious monody on the great wife of the Marchese di Pescara. Here is an exquisite stanza :

" ' For death, that breaks the marriage band
   In others, only closer pressed
   The wedding-ring upon her hand
   And closer locked and barred her breast.'

The memory of this noble lady, whom the Italians
call Divine, is further honored among the sonnets of
Michael Angelo, of which Mr. Longfellow has translated seven, two of which are addressed to her.
'The Revenge of Rain-in-the-Face' recalls the younger Mr. Longfellow of the hexameters 'To the Driving Cloud' and the brook-like measure of 'The
Song of Hiawatha.'   It celebrates better than any
other poem that we have seen the destruction of the
White Chief with the yellow hair and all his men in
the fatal snare into which Sitting Bull entrapped
them.

"The three following poems are on French and
Spanish themes, the most spirited being 'A Ballad of
the French Fleet.'   The time of the last is 1746; the
occasion the threatening of Boston by a French fleet,
which is scattered and sunk by a great October storm,
that was prayed for in the Old South Church by
the narrator of the incident, Mr. Thomas Price, whose
stern Puritan character, as shown in the ballad, is
strongly drawn.   'The Leap of Roushan Beg' is
a vivid seizure of the tumultuous life of a great bandit
chief, and of his perilous escape from his pursuers.
He had a wonderful horse, over whom he had the
most perfect control, and who obeyed his wish as he
obeyed his own will, leaping with him across a yawning mountain chasm thirty feet wide and landing

him safely on the further side. Here is a magnificent stanza of this great poem :

> " ' Roushan's tasselled cap of red
> Trembled not upon his head,
> Careless sat he and upright ;
> Neither hand nor bridle shook,
> Nor his head he turned to look,
> As he galloped out of sight.'

" 'Haroun-al-Raschid' is one of those apologues
which the Eastern poets are so fond of relating, and
of which Hunt's 'Abou-Ben-Adhem' is perhaps the
best example. The lesson which the poet teaches the
great Caliph is the old, sad lesson of mortality :

> " ' O thou who choosest for thy share
> The world, and what the world calls fair,

> " ' Take all that it can give or lend,
> But know that death is at the end!'

" 'The Three Kings' is a fresh and picturesque
handling of the beautiful old tradition of the Three
Wise Kings of the East (sometimes called the Three
Kings of Cologne), Melchior, Gaspar, and Baltasar,
and how they followed the star to Bethlehem. The
little song beginning 'Stay, stay at home, my heart,
and rest,' is the best lyric that Mr. Longfellow has
written since 'The Rainy Day,' which sang itself into
the world's remembrance nearly forty years ago. The
child was, indeed, the father of the man ; but in the
case of Mr. Longfellow the father is much greater

and broader and wiser than the child gave promise of being.

"The hero of 'The White Czar' is Peter the Great, who figures in the popular songs of the Russian people as *Batyuska* (Father dear) and *Gosudar* (sovereign). His spirit has arisen, and declares that the ships of his successors, which he thinks are his ships, shall sail to the Pillars of Hercules—a prophecy which may yet be fulfilled. There is a martial ring to the poem which is very effective, and which closes this section of the book like the blast of a trumpet.

"'A Book of Sonnets' contains twenty-two of Mr. Longfellow's exercises in that 'scanty plot of ground.' Mr. Longfellow, like Mr. Bryant, showed no aptness for writing sonnets in the earlier collections of his verse; but of late years he has cultivated this charming specialty with great care, and with perfect success. He has mastered all the laws which govern the body and soul of the legitimate Italian sonnet, and is to-day the finest living sonneteer. He does not attempt the grandiose and the magnificent, but confines his genius within the range of its sympathies, which are generous, and tender, and spiritual thoughts and things, with the serious mysteries of life and death and the world to come. If I were called upon to name the most imaginative poem that Mr. Longfellow has ever written, I should select the four sonnets which celebrate 'Two Rivers'—the rivers being those of Yesterday and To-morrow. There is a largeness and a strangeness in these sonnets which defies analysis, and is very remarkable.

"The last section of the volume is devoted to 'Translations,' of which there are fifteen. In the first two of these—'Virgil's First Eclogue' and 'Ovid in Exile'—Mr. Longfellow returns to his old love, the hexameter, which rewards his affection better than 'Evangeline.' I am inclined to think his last hexameters the best yet written by an American poet. I still regard the hexameter, however, as an experiment in English poetry, and I doubt its ultimate triumph. There are, in addition to those I have named, three translations from the French and two from the German, and translations of Michael Angelo's sonnets, and one of his canzones. Mr. Longfellow is easily the master of all translators into English poetry, and the specimens of his powers here are among the best that he has given us."

"CAMB., May 19, 1878.

"DEAR MR. STODDARD: Accept my thanks for your generous notice of 'Keramos' in the *Independent*, which I have read with pride and pleasure.

"I am never indifferent, and never pretend to be, to what people say or think of my books. They are my children, and I like to have them liked.

"When I send you the volume of 'Poems of Places' containing China, which I will do as soon as it is published, I hope you will not think I have taken too many of your 'Chinese Songs.'

"For these, also, I thank you. They have helped me greatly in that part—"

The hiatus which occurs here (made probably by

the pilfering fingers of some autograph-hunter) reminds me of the hiatus at the unfinished conclusion
of "Thealma and Clearchus," and the quaint words
of honest old Izaak Walton, who edited John Chalk-
hill's MSS.: "*And here the author died, and I hope
the reader will be sorry.*"

Before this reaches the reader the June number
of the *Century* magazine will no doubt have fallen
under his eye, and he will have read the following
note from the pen of its editor, Mr. Richard Watson
Gilder. It was dated at Shanklin, Isle of Wight,
October 1, 1879. Shanklin is a more famous locality
than Mr. Gilder remembered when he was there, for
it was there that John Keats and Charles Armitage
Brown resided after the former had finished his
"Eve of St. Agnes," and it was there that he wrote
his tragedy of "Otho the Great," and no doubt projected his "King Stephen":

"Just look at this group of thatched cottages!
The one on the right is a library where we go for
books. In the middle is the Crab Inn. Do you see
what looks like a pile of stones to the right of it?
That is a fountain for the use of the public. I read
some verses painted there on a piece of tin, and said
to myself: 'That must be from Longfellow.' I found
afterwards that they were written by him, by request,
when he was here, some years ago:

> " ' O Traveller, stay thy weary feet;
> Drink of this fountain pure and sweet;
> It flows for rich and poor the same.
> Then go thy way, remembering still
> The wayside well beneath the hill,
> The cup of water in His name.' "

From a manuscript copy of this little inscription I learn that it was written on July 21, 1868, and that Mr. Longfellow afterwards substituted "cool" for "pure" in the second line.

When I entered my office on the morning of Friday, March 24, I was handed a despatch from Boston which had been waiting for me, and which announced the death of Mr. Longfellow, and was asked to write an editorial upon it. As it was near noon, the editorial was necessarily brief. In the evening of the same day the editor of the *Tribune* asked me to furnish him with a column letter for the next morning's paper. I did the best I could under the circumstances. Another gentleman did much better under the same circumstances, for about the time that I was writing in New York my good friend Mr. Charles G. Whiting was writing in Springfield, in the office of the *Republican*, and writing after his day's work was thought to be finished, hurrying for dear life to have his editorial in the next morning's paper. The next day he wrote another editorial, either for the paper of the following day, or the day after. I have printed only one communication. It is from a young lady who prefers to be known only by her initials. I believe I need say no more, or need only say that the address which will follow this communication was read by me on the fore-noon of April 2; that the letters by which that is followed were written, at my request, by singular good friends of mine; and that the verse which closes all wrote itself in six hours on the evening and in the night and morning of the day of Mr. Longfellow's interment.

And here the author ends, and I hope the reader will be sorry.

On the midnight of the twenty-sixth day after the celebration of his seventy-fifth birthday throughout the civilized world the most fortunate and honored of all the English poets since Shakespeare, Henry Wadsworth Longfellow, began to enter into the shadow of the Invisible World. He was surrounded by those he loved best, dear children, hosts of worshipping friends, the great memory of Washington, and the best wishes of all good men and women. No passing away could be more felicitous than his. The haste with which this paragraph must be written prevents any—the least allusion to the many splendid intellectual achievements of this largely-gifted man, who illustrated all known literatures in the spirit of their original creators. He was the first American to introduce his countrymen to the treasure-house of German letters, to the abundant wealth of Spanish and Portuguese song and fable, to the awful kingdom of the stern old Florentine and his gentle Roman Master, to the glorious domain of the Golden Legend, the primitive poetry of Hiawatha and his beloved Minnehaha, to the grim Puritan ancestry of the New England of which we are so humbly proud, to the universe of human emotion and tenderness. Craigie House is henceforth doubly haunted. Two gracious Presences are now pacing its shining chambers, and the race is poorer from their departure. Master of sovran spirits.—*Ave atque Vale.*

MARCH 24.

(Tribune Editorial.)

TO THE EDITOR OF THE TRIBUNE:

SIR: I made my first acquaintance with the poetry of Mr. Longfellow at a much later period than I should have done, several years after I was familiar with the noble verse of his early master—the master of all of us—Bryant, and about the time that Mr. Edgar Allan Poe, his bitterest enemy, published "The Raven." It was in a cheap reprint of the "Voices of the Night," by the Harpers—a double-column paged pamphlet, dated somewhere in the fourth decade of the present century. It was, as nearly as I can recollect, in my twentieth year, which would be nearly at the time of the Langley-Matthews republication of the Poetical Works of Miss Elizabeth Barrett Barrett. I read it carelessly, as young people are apt to read metrical writing, and I did not under-

stand it as I might have done. I could not perceive
the delicate grace of the correspondences in the
" Prelude "—that airy fantasy in which substance
and shadow, body and soul, play at hide-and-seek,
reminding one of

> " The swan that on St. Mary's Lake
> Floats double, swan and shadow."

Whether the peculiar structure of this poem originated with Mr. Longfellow, or was borrowed by him
from some romantic German master—Uhland, perhaps, or Heine—I am not scholar enough to know.
It is a very dangerous form of composition, as the
readers of "The Reaper and the Flowers," "The
Beleaguered City," and " Midnight Mass for the Dying Year" could not fail to discover. How exquisite
it could be, in more skilful hands, they felt a few
years later when they read "The Rainy Day,"
" Maidenhood," and "The Arrow and the Song"—
which last perfect lyric has always flown into the
hearts of poets, making its divinest flight into the
heart of the greatest of her sex—Mrs. Browning. It
is the finest bay-leaf in the crown of young Mr. Longfellow that he was learned enough, while a professor
at Bowdoin, to transmute into his own charming English the El Dorado of several Continental literatures
—the weighty solemnity of Don Jorge Manrique, the

tender loveliness of Lope de Vega, the heavenliness
of De Aldana and De Medrano, and, later still, the
sacred Vision of the "Celestial Pilot" in the "Pur-
gatorio," and the blessedness of the holy Beatrice—
"*Manibus o date lilia plenis.*"

Lighter and darker strains succeeded, from Charles
d'Orleans, from the Anglo-Saxon, from stout Danish
Ewald, and from Tiedge, Müller, Uhland, and Sa-
lis.   Professor Longfellow transplanted the choicest
flowers of the German Tempe into his (and Bryant's)
own green land of groves.   All this while poor Edgar
Allan, unhappy, unsuccessful, with a sick wife, and a
demon struggling in his shattered soul, was reviling
Mr. Longfellow and other plagiarists in the *Mirror,*
the *Broadway Journal,* and every other periodical
into which he could thrust his envenomed stylus,
and was exhausting his purchased praises of certain
literary ladies, who shall be nameless, since they have
long since joined our vanished race of Sapphos and
Estelles.   And all this while his sovran in song and
the virtues forgave him.   "I never blamed him," he
wrote in substance, in a note which I have mislaid,
"for he was suffering and sorrowful, and he thought
me prosperous and happy."   It was so with all of us,
O my brothers of the *genus irritabile*—we were en-
vious of him, we were jealous of his superior powers
and place in the world's regard, and he heeded it not :

he knew beforehand all our calamities, how we begin
in gladness (as the great Master sings) and end—so
many of us end—in madness.   Pardon the least of
thy followers, loving and illustrious Spirit.

> " For there shall come a mightier blast,
>   There shall be a darker day ;
>   And the stars, from heaven downcast,
>   Like red leaves be swept away !
>   Kyrie eleison !
>   Christe eleison ! "

But all this, though heartfelt, is from my present
purpose, which is simply to jot down the little—it
is not much—that I know of Henry Wadsworth
Longfellow.   I paid him my first visit between thirty and forty years ago.   It was a bright, hot summer day, and he was living with his family, his
stately wife and his gentle children, in a house
which he had at Nahant.   It was, as I remember,
perched upon a bold and precipitous cliff, abrupt
and steep to the slip of sand which separated it
from the tumbling wall of surf, which was the wild-
est that I, almost sea-born, had ever seen.   I was the
obscurest of the obscure ; he the most gracious of
men.   With me was my good friend Fields, who
has passed before us into the Silent Land, and my
living friend, if he will let me call him such, Whip-

ple. We walked, the Knight and his squires and pages, across some fields, and the youngest of the last asked him if he remembered a certain image of Bryant's, but he had forgotten it. "It can be found," I said, "in 'After a Tempest,'" and I quoted the lines I had in mind, for I never forgot my Bryant :

> 'And darted up and down the butterfly,
> That seemed a living blossom in the air.'"

He nodded his head like one who was well pleased. "He made a note of that," said James Thomas, as we sauntered slowly behind. We went to dinner soon afterward. I sipped a little Lafitte, which I never liked, and the host told of his fancy for absurd books, some of which he had with him. I recollect that in one the hero bolted the door—and then bolted himself ! I dare say he had a case full of Columbiads, Fredoniads, Powhatans, Yamoydens, Milford Bards, Alonzo Lewises, and other dead and gone old Dunces. "Rest, perturbed spirits, rest !"

Some time later—I have no memory for dates—I called upon him, on another summer day, at Cambridge. I walked up the stately entrance to Craigie House, and was at once admitted, was shown into an ante-room lined with books, and, the family being at dinner, a glass of wine was sent to me until the

host could leave his guests. In a moment I was seated at his table, as I had lately been on the seashore,
surrounded by his children, and a gossiping chat
went round. What was it about? I could sooner
recall what song the Sirens sung to Ulysses, what ditty Marsyas piped before Apollo, what tune Achilles
whirled out of his distaff, or what courtly dance
Charmian trod before the Herculean Roman and the
serpent of old Nile, than that midsummer medley
over the walnuts and the wine. I dare say it was
something like this:

> " Care, like a dun,
> Lurks at the gate;
> Let the dog wait."

Or more like this, in *esse*, if not in *posse :*

> " Forty times over let Michaelmas pass,
> Grizzling hair the brain doth clear;
> Then you know a boy is an ass,
> Then you know the worth of a lass,
> Once you have come to Forty Year."

I met, or rather saw, Mr. Longfellow thrice again.
Once at the Old Corner Bookstore haunted with
memories of Ticknor, Fields, Hawthorne, Holmes,
Whittier, Emerson, Sumner, and Taylor—more glo-
rious memories of those immortal boys, William
Makepeace and Charles, and, I fear, dwindling

memories of several youngsters in the A's, and
H's, and J's, and L's—but of this meeting only the
shadow of a gracious Presence remains.   The next
time we met was at the Brunswick, where some
winter forenoon lang syne we gathered to do hon-
or to the first of Friends, singer of New England's
legendary lore, a good gray head which all men
knew—(hail, John Greenleaf Whittier !)—and where
the Poet of "The Golden Legend" welcomed me
with his clear eye and reverent beard, the Nestor
then of our bards—Nestor, but younger than Bryant
by over twelve years.   The third and last time I
heard of, but saw not, Longfellow, who came stealing
into Sanders Theatre on a hot June forenoon to hear
a certain rhapsodist essay a poem upon History before the young scholars of his beloved Alma Mater,
but came late, for the sly wag of a poet contrived to
go before the learned divine who strove for an hour
and a half to reconcile our Science and his Canadian
Orthodoxy.   Futile propounder of Paradoxes, I pit-
ied thee !   Two dear to me saw the venerable figure
gliding in and out, but the man he so honored beheld
him not, nor ever again.

I might have seen Longfellow two weeks ago, but I
had not the heart to disturb his age.   I remembered
the melancholy death of our great Commander of the
"Flood of Years," and broke not his peace.   Gene-

rally speaking, I come to praise Cæsar, not to bury him. What more need I say of the Man and his Work? Only what he said of our dear friend Hawthorne:

> " Ah! who shall lift that wand of magic power
>   And the lost clew regain?
> The unfinished window in Aladdin's tower
>   Unfinished must remain!"

New York, March 24, 1882.

THE POET LONGFELLOW DEAD.

(Springfield Republican.)

Henry Wadsworth Longfellow, the best-beloved of American poets, and the most widely read not only of American but of all living poets, died on Friday afternoon at his home in Cambridge, having survived not quite a month the hearty celebration all over his country of his seventy-fifth birthday. Mr. Longfellow has been growing physically feebler with the infirmities of age for the last two or three years, and finally yielded to an attack of peritonitis of several days' duration. Thus closes a life wholly valuable and beneficent in all its relations, and one of the early forces of our literature, that half a century ago was active, and yet was vital still in his last year of life.

Longfellow was born of a sturdy English ancestry, the old Puritan stock, unblent with other strains, and notable from its first entrance in the New World. The first of the name in this country was William Longfellow, who came from the English Hampshire in 1651 and settled in Newbury, where he married a sister of Chief-Justice Sewall, and who was wrecked with a boat's crew of the unlucky expedition of Sir William Phipps on its retreat from Quebec in 1690. His widow was left with six children, and one of them, named Stephen (after Stephen Dummer, grandfather of Mrs. Anne Sewall Longfellow), became a blacksmith. A recent novelist has made a college professor shrink with repulsion from a young man he has warmly befriended, when he learns the man's father was a blacksmith. But Longfellow the poet had nothing of this snobbery, and must have thought of his grandfather's grandfather when he wrote of the village blacksmith, who

> "—looks the whole world in the face,
>   For he owes not any man."

The blacksmith Longfellow married well, a minister's daughter of Marshfield, Abigail Thompson; and their son Stephen, who graduated from Harvard in 1742, became the schoolmaster of Portland, Me., and there remained through life, serving the community in many offices, such as town clerk, register of probate, etc. His oldest son, another Stephen, was important, too, in Gorham, where he lived, and whence he went eight years as representative in the General Court of Massachusetts ; moreover, he was justice of the Court of Common Pleas in Portland from 1797 to 1811. His son Stephen, the poet's father, was a distinguished lawyer, a member of the Hartford convention of New England federal disunionists in 1814, and member of the Eighteenth Congress. He married Zilpah, daughter of Gen. Peleg Wadsworth, and through her ancestry it was that Longfellow traced his descent to John Alden and Priscilla Mullins of the *Mayflower*. The poet was born February 27, 1807, in a large, square wooden house still standing in Portland, and was named Henry Wadsworth after his mother's brother, a lieutenant in the United States navy, who three years before in the harbor of Tripoli had given his life to his country in an attempt to destroy the Barbary pirate flotilla. This is the record of the race from which Longfellow the poet sprang to crown it with fame—a steady, serious, conscientious race, of more than average ability, so that their fellow-citizens commonly found it wise to employ them in public affairs ; with a finer strain about them, too, than about their neighbors, for we find that one Longfellow after another is noted as "gentle." The poet is a true practical as well as moral inheritor from his forefathers, for there have been no vagaries in his life, but a faithful and continuous service of his fellows ; but the poetic gift, which we find no trace of among them, must have come from the mother, where the characterizing quality of genius is so like to dwell. Thus we come to the career of Henry Wadsworth Longfellow.

In a home where honor and fortune and accomplishment were fortunately united the poet grew up. He began rhyming early, and the few poems of his boyhood that have been given to the world— only two or three besides those he has included in his collected "Poems"—testify to the inevitable course of his poetic bent. He was a poet at thirteen, and might as well have stopped breathing as rhyming. He was quick in all his intellectual processes, and entered Bowdoin College at the age of fourteen, in the same class with his elder brother, Stephen. This class, that of 1825, was the most distinguished one that was ever graduated from Bowdoin, and preserves the fame of the college. Its great stars are Longfellow and Hawthorne, but John S. C. Abbott, George B. Cheever, and Jonathan Cilley, the brilliant politician who fell in a meaningless duel with Graves of Kentucky, were also members ; Franklin Pierce, afterward President, was in the class preceding.   Longfellow excelled in all studies, and easily took class honors, graduating second among thirty-seven with an English oration on "Native Writers."   This, together with other literary work of his during his college life, led to his election to the newly established chair of modern languages and literature in less than a year after his graduation, and when he was but nineteen years old.   He left his father's law-office for Europe, and spent three years and a half in study of the principal European languages ; and probably an equal term of study never resulted in more excellent general preparation.   In a year from his entering upon his duties as professor his reputation was a magnet to attract students to Brunswick.   In 1833 his first published work appeared, "Coplas de Manrique," a translation of the lament of a young Spanish knight on his father's death, and one of the noblest of elegiac poems, which was prefaced by an essay on the moral and devotional poetry of Spain.   During this period he contributed to the *North American Review*, and published his "Outre-Mer," a book of travel.   In 1835 Mr. Longfellow was called to succeed George Ticknor as Professor of Modern Languages and Liter-

ature in Harvard College, and he again visited
the Old World, especially to study the languages
of northern Europe. During this residence abroad
his wife, the daughter of Judge Barrett Potter, of
Portland, whom he had married in 1831, died at
Rotterdam, and he finished his work under the burden of this first great sorrow. The shadow of it
tinges the pages of "Hyperion," the most exquisite of prose-poems, which was published in 1839.
Mr. Longfellow entered upon his duties as professor
at Harvard in 1836, and held the position for seven-
teen years, resigning then to live a purely literary
life. He made another visit to Europe in 1842, and
in 1845 published "The Poets and Poetry of Europe," one of the finest literary cyclopædias, not only
in the choice and the translation of representative
poetry, but in biographical and critical comment,
that has ever been made.

In 1843 Mr. Longfellow married again, his bride
being Frances Elizabeth Appleton (the Mary Ashburton of "Hyperion"), daughter of Nathan Appleton, of Boston, and bought the Craigie House
at Cambridge, the Washington headquarters, where
Edward Everett and Jared Sparks had lived before him. Here he has lived ever since ; here his
children, two sons and three daughters, were born ;
and here his lovely wife met her sudden and dread-

ful death by fire, her flowing sleeves catching flame
from a lamp in an evening entertainment with the
children. For her the poet remained a mourner to
his death. The years continued to be fruitful in
literary work, his volumes of verse following each
other at short intervals, the most noted coming thus :
"Voices of the Night," 1839 ; "The Spanish Student," 1843 ; "Evangeline," 1847 ; "The Golden Legend," 1851 ; "The Song of Hiawatha," 1855 ; "The
Courtship of Miles Standish," 1858 ; "Tales of a
Wayside Inn," 1863 ; "The New England Tragedies," 1868 ; "The Divine Tragedy," 1872 ; and
"Aftermath," in 1873. Notwithstanding the sad
finality of this last title, the poet was fortunately
wrong, for he has plucked from his hearth and fields
since then "The Hanging of the Crane," 1874 ; "The
Masque of Pandora," 1875 ; "Keramos," 1878 ; and
"Ultima Thule," 1880—even since this last we have
had some worthy grain from him, not to speak of
his admirable editorial work in the selection of
"Poems of Places," which in thirty-one volumes
comprises a wonderful variety of fine verse. Within
a year, also, a superb subscription edition of all his
poetical works has been issued in this country
and England, illustrated by the principal artists of
America.

Mr. Longfellow has received abundant honors in

his own country and abroad : Harvard made him
LL.D. in 1859, and both Oxford and Cambridge gave
him the degree of D.C.L. on his latest visit to England and the Continent, in 1868-9. But his true honors have been the adoption of his poems into many
other literatures ; all the languages of Europe, and
some of Asia, have given his verse a new public in some
degree, and "Evangeline," "Hiawatha," "The Gold-
en Legend," "The Spanish Student" especially have
been made familiar. The sale in America of Longfellow's works during the first sixteen years of his au-
thorship numbered 325,550 copies, 293,000 of which
were poetical and 32,550 prose. Since then no one has
taken the trouble to compute, but the popularity of
Longfellow, far from waning, has steadily increased.
No other poet of to-day, it is safe to say, has reached
anything like the number of readers, or touched so
universally the chords of human sympathy, as Longfellow has. All this time he has remained a modest,
noble, sweet-hearted gentleman, untouched by vanity, clear of pretension, certain of his mission ; a centre of interest in the literature of America, and to the
literary men and women of all countries who visit
America ; loved in thousands of households where he .
must remain unknown except by his verse ; and an
unending influence for beauty in life, and all the surroundings of life.

HIS QUALITY AS POET.

Longfellow, in the foreign estimation, holds the highest place among all the names of our literature. He was one of the first to catch the attention of English critics, and they have clung to him as to a sheet-anchor in the overwhelming rush of American writers since. They are fond of calling him "America's greatest literary son," because such an attribution would restrict our literature to a certain level of excellence which without doubt has been far exceeded by others of our authors. This has occasioned a perceptible reaction among home critics, and perhaps caused them to depreciate the real merit of Longfellow. It will be agreed that he is not a poet of the first, or even of the second, order. He cannot rank with Emerson, or with Tennyson and Browning. Not the exalted treasure of celestial thought, not the dramatic power of intense passions, not the mystic subtlety of refined ideals, is his. But the chords of daily human experience, the level beauty of common life, the sense of content and of grief, the imaginative picturing of legend and allegory—these he knew well. He was never false in a word or a form of words. His lyre sang true every note, whether in major or minor keys. All humanity responds to its music, and that music is exquisite. There is a great variety in his work, yet he has not written anything without the charm that indicates poetry. He has never been a sloven in his verse; while at the same time he has never wandered in search of mechanical elaboration, as the fashion has been since Swinburne scared the whole guild of English writers by his exhaustive gymnastics with the entire resources of the language. Without any fantastic devices of rhythm and metre, he never failed in fitting his form to his thought, and is justly to be called a master in the mechanism of poesy. The hexameters of "Evangeline," the trochaics of "Hiawatha," the blank verse of "The New England Tragedies" and "Christus," owe their charm to their fitness to the burdens they bear. "Hiawatha," for instance, although its metre is the same as that of the Finnish epic "Kalevala," is as close an echo of the movement of Indian song as could be attained in verse—at times it is like an inspiration of the prairies and forests which are the scenes of the legends. And while the tremendous artifice of Swinburne will inevitably pall on the ear, and finally sink into the abyss of half-forgotten curiosities, Longfellow's pure and simple melody will live in perennial freshness, because it is sweet, unaffected, genuine, and, beyond all, because it conveys noble messages instead of ignoble.

Mr. Longfellow had a true and high poetic purpose, which he fulfilled. He was not an enthusiast for any one cause, but he had his aim fixed on the great family, to reach the feeling of men and women, ay, and children, so that they should find his verses household words, inspired with encouragement in urgent need, touched with sympathy in daily experience, and satisfying with consolation in defeat and sorrow. He is often called the poet of the commonplace, and this is not an unjust characterization, except as the critic's animus makes it so. Life is commonplace, even its worst and best features are constantly reproducing themselves, and it has been Longfellow's gift and glory to unite his verse to so many various phases of our experience, to associate his words with our pleasures and our griefs. The "Voices of the Night" have sounded in our ears, the "Psalm of Life" has come to our rescue repeatedly ; even if it be sometimes recited shallowly in jest, it is always inspiriting to say :

> " Let us, then, be up and doing,
>   With a heart for any fate ;
> Still achieving, still pursuing,
>   Learn to labor and to wait."

Is not this a worthy pilotage for life ? Time would fail to recall the poems wherein such help as this has been afforded his fellows by this poet. And where the higher fancy is stimulated, who offers freer-winged carriage than he in the wonderful music of "Sandalphon, the 'Angel of Prayer'"?—when

> " Serene in the rapturous throng,
>   Unmoved by the rush of the song,
>   With eyes unimpassioned and slow,
>   Among the dead angels the deathless
>   Sandalphon stands listening breathless
>   To sounds that ascend from below."

And the judgment of Lowell stands unimpeached on the poem of the Acadian maiden—

> " ——that rare, tender, virgin-like pastoral ' Evangeline,'
>   That's not ancient or modern; its place is apart
>   Where Time has no sway, in the realm of pure Art.
>   'Tis a shrine of retreat from earth's hubbub and strife,
>   As quiet and chaste as the author's own life."

Longfellow was such a translator as a poet would wish to have. A German or Swedish or Spanish poem in his hands became an English poem. But he was not successful in reproducing Dante. It is an evidence of his superiority to jealousy that he regarded Dr. Parsons as a better translator of Dante than himself, and once said that there was more of the great Italian in Parsons's lines on a bust of Dante

than in all his own version of the " Divina Commedia."

Longfellow was not peculiarly an American poet,
although he turned his attention to American themes.
His was—as the English said in the day when Sydney
Smith wanted to know who read an American book,
and when Lowell's Apollo declared that—

> " Our literature suits each whisper and motion
> To what will be thought of it over the ocean "

—an English mind, with the culture of Europe mould-
ing its utterances. He never lacked the essential moral sympathy with America, yet that sympathy never
became with him a flaming fire as with Whittier, or
a rapier-edge as with Lowell ; nor did he have that
grand sweep of external nature which set aside Bryant as the embodiment of the American scene, or the
inimitable brilliancy that marks Holmes so far in advance of contemporary England, or the shrewd union
of Yankee and orient genius that revealed a gospel in
Emerson. The scarcity of Longfellow's anti-slavery
and patriotic poems proves this lack of absolute Ame-
ricanism in the humanitarian aspect of his verse. But
he was emphatically a universal people's poet, and
gained a fame that will not fade so long as English
is spoken—an immortality of the good, the true, and
the beautiful.

In the point of character Longfellow possesses his finest strength. His soul was as clean as a child's through his whole life, and yet nowhere devoid of manly strength and fellowship. The work he did is the transcript of his nature to an extraordinary degree. Pure, inspiring purity, and rebuking grossness of life, like Arthur in his Round Table, was Longfellow. This has been a common characteristic of all our elder poets: of Bryant " the master of us all," as Stoddard calls him —of Emerson, Whittier, Holmes, Lowell, Bayard Taylor, Parsons. These have not only avoided coarseness and open sensuality, but they have not borne that insinuation of evil which is so common among the younger writers of the day. The same decadence is more noticeable, and far lower, in England than here. From Tennyson to Swinburne, from Browning to Dante Rossetti, is a great descent. And in the next younger poets we behold an array of boys trying verbal gymnastics in rondeaux, ballades, etc. In this country there is as yet less artifice, but there is also less sign of any genius at all.

There arise in our poetical horizon no poetic stars of great magnitude. We have an abundance of men and women who, sometimes strongly, sometimes daintily, strike the lyre of song, but it is a grave question whether our first poetic era be not now at an end, and

its successor not yet dawned. The spontaneous note
is lacking among our songsters. There is a good deal
of fine singing, but it is singing that has been learned in school, and very imperfectly understood. It
would be invidious to mention the names of the
youngest men who may suddenly outburst in something new and worthy. There are yet those who
survive to set a great example : Holmes and Whittier, and their juniors, Lowell and Stoddard, and
Parsons, who writes too little for a poet of so fine
quality, and who rests his fame securely on his
translation of Dante, which still engages his labors.
Stedman has sunk the bard in the critic of late to
the great advantage of criticism ; Aldrich and How-
ells and Lathrop have become novelists ; Boyle
O'Reilly has allowed the editor to wreck the poet ;
and Walt Whitman stands alone—great, incompara-
ble, and unfollowed. The score or more of younger
men seem given over to fantasies and humors, and
poisoned by egotism. This last fault seems hopeless.
What can be done with a lot of youth who regard
their personal feelings as the supreme subject of their
verse, and drag their morbid notions into every phase
of thought, study of outer nature, or picture of
human life? How free from this dragging personality was Longfellow—how far above this low
self-consciousness, even in his deepest emotional

poems! He never became the centre of the poetic thought, for he was greater than his sole experience.

AN EVENING IN THE OLD CRAIGIE HOUSE.

To the Editor of the Tribune:

Sir: No face was better known or loved in Cambridge (alas! that we must say *was*) than the genial face of America's best-known poet, Longfellow, with its silvery crown of radiant white hair. His brown overcoat, too, was as well known and almost as historical, though for a far different reason, as the gray redingote of the first Napoleon. But all the world has not been to Cambridge (though the Cantabrigians seem to think otherwise), and perhaps an account of an evening with the poet may pass over some ground hitherto untravelled.

It was in the winter of 1880 that I had the pleasure of first seeing Longfellow in his own home. I was a stranger in Cambridge, but there is nothing more charming and delightful than Cambridge hospitality. In the old Craigie Mansion on Brattle Street used to be free-hearted hospitality, and that hospitality received a fresh lease of life when the poet took up his

home there. I had been in Cambridge only a few
weeks when with two friends I was invited to dine
with Mr. Longfellow and spend the evening ; the in-
vitation was not for a dinner-party, but for a purely
informal meal, and was all the more welcome. It
was a moonlight night when we left our home and
walked down Brattle Street facing the Charles ; as
we entered the gate the old mansion stood trans-
figured in the moonlight, the river gleamed silver
white, the sheltering row of bare lilac bushes had a
spectral effect, which was enhanced by the two tall
poplars, bare and straight, standing like sentinels in
the quiet moonlight. But when we mounted the
steps, rang the bell of the old door with its quaint
brass knocker, and stepped inside the broad hall,
there was nothing unreal or unsubstantial in our
welcome. The bell was hardly touched when the
door swung open and we stepped into a hospitable
hall as large as an ordinary room, its walls hung
with paintings ; facing the door was the old-fashioned
broad staircase ; half-way up the stairs, on the first
landing. stood the tall clock, saying :

> " For ever, never;
> Never, for ever."

On the left of the entrance was the small reception-
room, and back of it the dining-room ; on the other

side was the historic study which has been so many
times described. In the rear of this was the large
drawing-room or library, into which we were ushered
after laying aside our wraps. The drawing-room was
cheery with red hangings; in the corner stood a large
grand piano, the walls were literally lined with book-
shelves, and in the centre of the room stood a table
bestrewn with books and papers. A cheery open
fireplace, whose yawning mouth was encircled by a
row of quaintly-colored tiles, and which gave forth
a genial warmth from a huge log crackling on some
curious brass andirons, added color and warmth to
the home picture. But why linger on the mere out-
side shell?   .

The door suddenly opened and Longfellow walked
in. He was rather shorter in stature than we had
anticipated, but very erect and vigorous; his frame
was neither stout nor thin; his face was ruddy in
complexion and surrounded by a mass of silvery
white hair; the eyes, surmounted by bushy eye-
brows, were the chief charm of the mobile face;
they looked out so bright and keen that it was difficult to tell their color, though it appeared to be
blue; we were inclined to be struck by the brilliancy
rather than the shade. Around the eyes were some
characteristic wrinkles, which gave a genial and happy expression to the face when the poet smiled. As

he entered there was a cordial grace and ease in his manner which put every one at ease. It is related that before Heine met Goethe he had prepared a fine speech to deliver, but when he saw the great man he could only stammer, "Ah! the plums are very fine on the road to Weimar." But one needed not to prepare a speech before meeting Longfellow; he himself was your inspiration. When you met him you felt you were with a friend; immediately "your dumb devil took leave of you."

After shaking hands with us all the poet laughingly said: "It is an embarrassment of riches--I'd offer my arm to one of you, but I don't know which!" So the six ladies went in arm-in-arm, Mr. Longfellow followed, and the company of seven sat down at the cheerful round table. On the wall at the left of the pleasant dining-room hung a large oil-painting of the three daughters of the poet; from this picture the photograph which is so popular has been taken. All through dinner-time the poet chatted and talked, flying like a bird lightly from branch to branch, and making whatever subject he lingered on cheerful and bright. He spoke of Carlyle, who was still alive, and praised him in very high terms. "I particularly admire his 'French Revolution' and 'Frederick the Great,'" he said; "I consider him as one of the few writers who have made history really live.   Carlyle saw facts with his imagination."

Then the poet gave some reminiscences of his college days at Bowdoin. "The study that I most disliked was Forensics," he continued. "I begged the president to excuse me, but, to my surprise, when the class came up I was the first one called upon to recite! I don't think the president was very fond of me. Some of our professors, too, were very amusing; one of them in Mental Science always began questioning us in this manner : 'Now, young gentlemen, what is logic; or, in the words of the author, logic is what?' I did not care so much for the mere bare facts of Mental Science; I loved them clothed in appropriate words. Do you remember this fine quotation from John Locke : 'Thus the ideas, as well as children, of our youth often die before us; and our minds represent to us those tombs to which we are approaching where, though the brass and marble remain, yet the inscriptions are effaced by time and the imagery moulders away'?" Then he solemnly added : "God grant that I may be preserved from that!" The prayer has been granted, and he has been taken from us while still strong and able to bear the poet's message to humanity.

Soon after reciting this passage the conversation turned to poets and poetry. "Dante is a transcendent poet," said his translator, and then recited in Italian a portion of the opening canto of the "Inferno." "Can anything be more simple and direct than that, and yet more musical and full of thought?" he asked. "It is easy enough to be simple at the expense of beauty," he added, "or to be musical at the expense of thought; the great poet is the man who, at a white heat, welds simplicity with beauty, and thought with music."

After dinner the ladies retired to the drawing-room; about half an hour later Longfellow entered and turned over the bound pages of *Vanity Fair*, a periodical filled with caricatures of different celebrated men. All the time he was turning the leaves there flowed forth a running commentary of wit, memories, and anecdotes which it is as impossible to describe as it would be to picture by words a mountain brook. Upon the mantel there was a beautiful photograph of a refined, delicate face. It was a man of about thirty-five apparently, with a fine broad forehead, soft, silky hair brushed carelessly back, dark, dreamy eyes, and an exquisitely chiselled mouth and chin. "I am glad you like the photograph," said the poet to me. "It represents my dear friend Ruskin at his best. I met Ruskin first in Paris. His manner was very quiet, gentle, and mild, but tinged with deep melancholy; it was just after his domestic trouble. His first words on meeting me were, ' Sir, you know I hate Americans ! ' but he said it with such a gentle smile and manner I could not take offence. ' Very well, sir,' I replied. From that time we were firm friends. When I saw him for the last time he said to me : ' It's very strange ; I cannot understand it ! I hate Americans, and yet you, Mr. Longfellow, and Mr. Norton, both Americans, are the only two men with whom I feel thoroughly happy, sympathetic, and at ease.' After our first meeting in Paris I met Ruskin again at Verona, a city which I admire greatly. I stopped by chance at the same hotel with him, ran across his valet one morning, and told him to ask his master to come down to table-d'hôte. ' I never go to table-d'hôte,' was the response ; but he came in to see me later, and we spent a charming evening together. Next day we drove around Verona and visited the amphitheatre together. A few days later I saw him busily sketching away in the Piazza della Erba, while his valet was holding a crowd of Italian lazzaroni at bay. The last time I saw Ruskin he was perched on top of a ladder in front of the grand monument to Can Grande, sketching in some architectural details. I am afraid that Ruskin's love for detail leads him to overlook breadth ; for instance, he took me to a little church in Verona, where the one thing he singled out as worthy of admiration was a small twisted pillar mounted on a griffin's back! Ruskin has really a wonderful fondness for delicacy of effect and fineness, however. He has a thoroughly sensitive, fine nature, which demands thoroughness in the least. His manner, courteous, refined, with the old-school politeness which is fast passing away in our rough and hurried life, is most charming."

After leaving Ruskin the conversation flowed lightly on around other topics. "I hate parodies," said the poet warmly. "A man who parodies a good poem ought to be hanged—metaphorically, of course," he added quickly. "I do not mind critics or criticism so much. A man's best critic should be himself. You generally believe a critic only when he agrees with you. But it is much more important to make your life fit your own standard than theirs. The great struggle of a poet should be toward originality."

In a short discussion upon American novelists he said: "I cannot see how —— can place so much value upon mere bric-à-brac; those things are the trappings of art, the stage properties merely. Did it vitally matter to Hawthorne that there were no castles in America? The true life is the life of the soul, and not of the body; within our four walls lies our home; all of human life lies in the home. America, having this, has all that the richest nation in the world could desire.'

So the conversation flowed on ; but who can reproduce its thousand felicities, its cheeriness, its breadth, its kindliness and world-wide sympathy ? What has been given is the mere shadow of the past ; let those who love the poet take it as it was meant—an attempt to throw a single flower, dwarfed though it may be, upon the newly-made grave of that loved poet whom the whole world delights to honor !   E. A. T.

BROOKLYN, April 7, 1882.

THERE were memorial addresses before the Society for Ethical Culture in the forenoon of April 2. The following is an account of the services, which were begun by Professor Felix Adler :

PROF. FELIX ADLER :

Our platform is graced to-day by the presence of a poet whose name is familiar and dear to many thousands in this land. To such a one it behooves us to show honor and respect in all things. I shall do so now by respecting the wish which he has uttered, that I may be wholly brief in presenting him to this audience. Mr. Richard H. Stoddard

will now address you on the Poet and the Divine
Poetic Art.

MR. RICHARD H. STODDARD'S ADDRESS.

I have been asked to speak for a few minutes
about Mr. Longfellow, but not so much about him
personally as about the choir of poets to which he
belonged, and the place that the faculty which he
and they possess, and possessed, holds among the
endowments of the race. It is not with the Man,
or the Men, that I propose to detain you, but with
the genesis of his, and their, Work. He was one
of many—but not so many, after all—who were
gifted with powers that are not common to the generations of mankind. Why they were so gifted no
man knows, and of the source of their powers all
must remain ignorant. It is one of the mysteries
that surround us, perhaps the heart of the dear-
est, as the Infinite Unknown of our poor human
speech is the soul of the profoundest—the creative
energy which we call Father. The first poet was
the first man who was conscious of himself and of
the Universe—the childly-hearted creature of whom
the twinkle of a dewdrop, the delicate grace of a
spring blossom, or the fingers of the wind that dal-
lied with his hair made a lyrical singer; to whom
the surf sang strophes of jubilance; the flash of

lightning and the crash of thunder were Ode and Epode of a mighty measure ; moonlights epithalamia, and darkness the pall of the tragedy of the Unknowable. When he opened his eyes to the glory and the terror that were about him he was a poet. If we could recall our childish conceptions of these we might recall the voices that awakened his spirit, the apparitions that beckoned to and eluded it. The earliest message that approached his ear from the lips of Nature was half inaudible and of uncertain import. He knew not whether to be delighted or afraid. He was aware of another and a stronger than himself—of something above him, below him, within him, from Whom he could not escape, a perpetual environment and fulfilment —the Maker securing the made. So far as they can be traced, the primitive utterances of man were a recognition of Power, which speedily became powers, which assumed names, and were clothed upon by shadowy, elemental, fleshly shapes—adumbrations of their worshippers projected against the wall of the worlds. Man made his gods, in his own image, but superior, for good and evil ; and as he made them, so they remain to-day—the good, let us hope, trampling the evil under foot. The oldest poems extant are invocations to deities—orphic hymns that strove to capture and detain their singers hardly knew what, to translate the original language of encircling Presences into the dialects of barbaric tribes; confessions of transgression and supplications for forgiveness; mortal acknowledgments of the divine, like those in the Sacred Book of the Hebrews: "Lord, what is man that thou art mindful of him, or the son of man that thou visitest him?" Such were these old forgotten poets, and such their strains in the morning of Time.

While the spiritual needs of man were demanding those rhythmic recognitions, his physical needs were demanding their recognition in stormier music —in the rugged songs that narrated his encounters with savage beasts, and in the short, sharp odes that strengthened his sinews to heave great rocks upon his foes, and to brain them with upwrecked forests —valorous, vindictive, victorious. The hands of Nimrod conquered in the one, the fires of Moloch consumed in the other, and the earth was darkened with the smoke of battle. From out this tumult stole fórth slowly, but surely, a Woman not seen before, stern, but sad and gracious, whose office it was to recover and embalm the memory of heroes, friends and foes, both noble, now they were gone; so just, so human, is the twin sister of song—Tradition. But back of all these shapes and sounds,

back of the soldier in battle and the gray-bearded
priest in sacred places, are beauteous shadows and
melodious voices, figures of youths and maids sitting upon banks of flowers, or stealing through
the twilight of secluded woods, whispering secrets,
exchanging hearts, clasping hands, looking immortal life, old-world lovers, singing the song that
never is old. Perhaps they touch rude instru-
ments, fetch music from string and shell, or up
and dance for utter joy; whatever they do, all's
well.

> " Be not-afeard ; the isle is full of noises,
>   Sounds, and sweet airs, that give delight and hurt not."

Through all these jocund ditties float, from vine-
yards where grapes are trodden into wine, from pro-
cessions along the highways crowned with vine-
leaves, with faces flushed, trumpets blowing, cym-
bals clashing, emptied cups and stumbling feet, passing away, the sons of Belial, Thammuz and the Syrian damsels, Bacchus and Silenus, poetic impersona-
tions of opulence and waste. Be sure that more than
revelry was meant in these, that hidden therein were
myths whose original meaning hath escaped us—
parables of the use and abuse of good, parents of
Saadi and Omar Khayyam.

" Why, be this juice the growth of God, who dare
  Blaspheme the twisted tendril as a snare ?
    A blessing we should use it, should we not ?
    And if a curse, why, then, who set it there ?"

The soul solicits wisdom. It is delivered by the poet. The limits of our vision and our set habits of mind narrow our knowledge and conceptions of poetry. Before Greece was, and her mighty mother, Egypt, there was a world of song. There were poets in the steppes of Scythia, in the defiles of the Himalayas, along the banks of the Niger, in the mines of Cornwall, in the endless forests of the unfound continent, on the surf-washed beaches of the Pacific, and over the sunken cities of the Atlantides—wherever mankind was, there were poets. Everywhere the fourfold stream of religion, and love, and war, and wine was flowing, and men and women rose and floated and sunk therein from of old, as they are rising and floating and sinking now. It sings about a thousand little islands peopled with lyrical birds ; it lapses gaily along the sunny shore of comedy ; it sets perpetually to the world where tragedy is, surrounded by lost lovers and unwedded maids, discrowned and unsceptred kings and queens. wan rulers of crushed empires weighed down with Fate. Whatever the race has been, is, or may be, that poetry has been, is, and must be. It is human life and death.

From the beginning it has broadened and deepened.
The simple worship of the world's forefathers shaped
itself into prayers, invocations, and mystic hymns—
the Vedas, the Zendavesta, the Theogony, the Hebrew Writings, and the Evangelists. The anger
of its children shaped itself into war-songs in all
lands, and into the epical ocean wherein they were
discharged—Iliads, Mahabharratas, Æneids, Divine
Comedies, Paradises Lost. The wine-bibbing of its
grandchildren shaped itself into satiric combats between rival wits, who set the rustics agape, and
whose torches reached us through the hands of
Aristophanes, Terence, Molière, and Shakespeare;
the sorrow and sullenness of all reaching us in
Prometheus, Medea, Antigone, gliding away in a
thousand pallid figures, to reappear as Hamlet, Lear,
Queen Katharine, Lady Macbeth. Amorists of antiquity reached us through the souls of Hero and
Leander, Dante and Beatrice,

" And many more the Muse may not rehearse."

Akin to these crying and laughing ones, were and
are, the shepherd-folk and countrymen of Theocritus,
Bion and Moschus, Keats and Tennyson. Such are
the dwellers in, and such the dominion of, Song,
whereof the Poet is Sovereign, Lord under the Great
Lord of the lesser universe. It is an awful sceptre

which he holds, this Porphyrogenitus, for the honor which accompanies it must be borne meekly, and the burden which it imposes is for life and death. He receives what the Giver sends, and gives it again—what, he knows not, save that it is good.

> " There is a soul of goodness in things ill,
> Would men observingly distil it out."

The divine light streams :

> " Life, like a dome of many-colored glass,
> Stains the white radiance of Eternity."

First-born of Nature, and more closely held to her heart than any of her children, the poet apprehends and comprehends the Universal Mother. What escapes the trained eye of the painter he instinctively discerns ; foreseeing the unseen light, and preventing the distant darkness, master of his moods and interpreter of her mysteries, she has no secrets from her darling! Wisdom whispers her oracles through him. He is the mouthpiece of wit, art, eloquence of words, purity of sculpture, glory of color, ineffable tenderness and might of music ; fourfold waters of the Unknown are the rivers of his Eden, before whose gates flames no fiery sword, for man has never been driven forth, but walks there at morn and eventide—familiar with the gods.

Such is the Poet, and such, within his limitations, was Longfellow, whom the world laments—most gracious of Puritans, beneficent flower from the stern old stem of John Alden.

PROF. FELIX ADLER:

The poet has spoken of poetry, as we have heard. It is for the appreciative critic to mark for us the distinctive merits of the bard whose loss we deplore to-day. No one is more competent to do this than Mr. Edwin P. Whipple, a name eminent in American literature. Mr. Whipple is prevented by indisposition from being with us to-day, and his address will be read by Mr. Charles Roberts, Jr., whose perfect delivery will form the beautiful vehicle for admirable thought.

MR. EDWIN P. WHIPPLE'S ADDRESS.

It was affirmed by one of the great poets of the century, who spoke from his inspired insight into the external world, that

> " They do not err
> Who say, that when a poet dies
> Mute Nature mourns her worshipper,
> And celebrates his obsequies."

Indeed, it is the Mind in this Nature—dumb, but neither deaf nor blind—that the poet interprets, and shows to be one with the Mind in human nature, happily gifted with an articulate voice. The death of a poet, therefore, as contrasted with that of the most eminent scientist, strikes us all as an abrupt withdrawal of one of those exceptional beings through whose vivid spiritual vision of the life of things we are enabled to catch glimpses of vital realities which are not revealed to the keenest scientific observation or the most patient scientific analysis.

In the case of the departure of Longfellow this sense of loss is deepened by our love and admiration of the character of the man. It was said, years ago, by a competent foreign critic, that there was something, he hardly knew what, in the poems of Longfellow which made them universally attractive; but those who personally knew the man readily understood what constituted the peculiar attractiveness of the poet. He was, in the first place, one of the humanest of men, utterly incapable of envy, malice, or intolerance, and gifted not only with the power of discerning merit in others, but of heartily rejoicing in its contemplation. Wherever he appeared he radiated the spirit of kindliness and beneficence. It was impossible to know him without feeling an affection for him. And he was very comprehensive in his humanity. It included sects and parties that hated and despised each other, and diversities of individual

character which were mutually repulsive. His toleration extended to the toleration of intolerance, even
when he himself was its victim.   Thus, when he
was vehemently denounced by some earnest abolitionists for that passage in "The Building of the
Ship" glorifying the Union of the States, he quietly
said to an indignant friend : "These men are justified
in attacking me. Knowing their opinions as I do,
they could not honestly act otherwise."

This breadth of sympathetic feeling gave variety to
the products of his genius.   It enabled him to reproduce many different moods of mind and many differerent forms of character. A glance over his poems
shows how wide is the field his writings cover. He
rarely, if ever, repeats himself. If we take his long
poems, such as "The Spanish Student," "The Golden Legend," "Hiawatha," "Evangeline," we wonder
how the same poet could have selected subjects so
different, and have treated each with such masterly
adaptation of his genius to his theme.   Our wonder is increased when we remember the throng of
lyrics and minor poems with which he has enriched
our literature, and the flexibility of mind he displays
in placing himself on an equality with every idea,
sentiment, situation, and topic he represents. In all
these the individuality of the man is constantly perceived, but the range of the genius is remarkable.

Perhaps the controlling element in his nature was the moral sentiment, and it is also the dominant quality observed in his writings. And his morality is the morality of most good men and women. He deals in no moral paradoxes, while he touches no moral truism without vitalizing it—without imparting to it a new life, freshness, elevation, beauty, and power. He thus finds his way into all self-respecting homes and is domesticated at all pure firesides. His extraordinary intensity of perception of ordinary feelings and beliefs is the chief source of his popularity.

The intellectual equipment of this fine nature was of exceptional excellence. He was a man of large and liberal scholarship, gifted with a creative and realizing mind. His learning, therefore, was all alive, connecting itself throughout its wide scope of accomplishment with suggested thoughts, emotions, pictures, and persons. And then consider his power of what may be called executive expression. His words and images always tell. He ever succeeds in conveying to another mind the matter that fills his own. It is impossible to miss his meaning, or fail to feel it as he feels it. Generally his style impresses us by the solidity and weight of its melodiously arranged words. In " The Arsenal at Springfield," " Seaweed," " Sand of the Desert," " The Occultation of Orion," "Sandalphon," "The Lighthouse," not to mention others, note the massiveness of the diction ! What a description is this of the effects of war :

> " The tumult of each sacked and burning village,
> The shout that every prayer for mercy drowns,
> The soldiers' revel in the midst of pillage,
> *The wail of famine in beleaguered towns.*"

How sound helps sense and imagination in this verse from "The Lighthouse":

> " The startled waves leap over it, the storm
> Smites it with all the scourges of the rain;
> And steadily against its solid form
> *Press the great shoulders of the hurricane.*"

Most of Longfellow's poems are characterized by this clearness, picturesqueness, and especially this weight of diction. The effect on the ear is as great as the effect on the eye. We instinctively read his most celebrated pieces aloud. When, as in "Endymion" and "Maidenhood," he succeeds in embodying sub-tile thoughts and melodies, we commonly find that he has failed in reaching his audience of fifty thousand readers. The most wonderful poem of this kind in modern English literature is Tennyson's "Echo Song" in "The Princess"—a lyric whose interior music has never been adequately rendered by the voice of any singer or elocutionist. Longfellow's efforts in this direction, though perhaps artistically his best, have never obtained popularity.

It would be difficult to state in a short address how many avenues Longfellow has opened to the popular heart and brain. The effect of all his writings is to purify as well as to please. Few whose sense of beauty was so keen have combined with it an ethical purpose so high. He belongs to that class of poets, we gratefully remember, who have quickened and strengthened conscience through kindling appeals to the emotions and imagination :

> " Filling the soul with sentiments august,
> The beautiful, the brave, the holy, and the just."

PROF. FELIX ADLER'S ADDRESS.

You may inquire in wonder why another word should be added to what has already been said. It was our wish to-day that the poet should speak to us of his noble art, and the distinguished critic point out the merits of our Bard. And amply has this wish been fulfilled in the words which you have heard. And yet I speak as one of many thousands who have derived a sweet and restful pleasure from the songs of the dead poet. And it is the desire to say my thanks, the simple impulse of gratitude, that prompts me to add my humbler tribute to what has already been said so much better.

The office of the poet is, indeed, a holy one. Sometimes he is both poet and prophet in one. Such a one Longfellow was not. But always he is both poet and priest in one : priest at the sacred shrine of the feelings. But you may think of certain ones who are known as poets, and may ask : Are these, too, to be classed as priests ? Yes ; for as there are false priests in religion, so there are false priests in poetry. There have been priests who converted their temples into temples of lust, and the ceremonies of religion into orgies of wild desire, and lifted up the senses upon the pedestals of the gods, and chained the soul upon the ground. So there are false priests in poetry at the present day—men who are filled with the wind of passion and drive lawlessly whithersoever the gusts of desire urge them on ; men who select what is base and foul in human nature to throw over it the glamour of their art, and who dip the golden goblets of poetry into the green morass to fill them with its rank and fetid waters. Such a one Longfellow was not. He was a white-robed priest—a priest clad in purity. Whatever his clean eyes saw became clean under his gaze ; whatever his fine hands seized became fine under his touch.

Secondly, it behooves us to mention the sympathy with which he responded to the life of nature and of man. He would not have been a poet, indeed, had he been devoid of such sympathy. And yet the quality of his sympathy, the tender pathos that thrills all through it, is peculiar to him. To all his singing may be applied what he himself said of his "Hiawatha": that every letter "is full of hope and yet of heart-break"; or what he causes Prince Henry to say in the "Golden Legend": "This life of ours is a wild Æolian harp of many a joyous strain, but underneath them all there runs a loud, perpetual wail, as of souls in pain." So underneath his verses there seems to run the wail as of a soul in pain. And yet sorrow with him was subdued, and grief did not prevent him from receiving into his heart every mood of nature, and giving forth again in song the echo of all her loveliness and her mystery. Whether he speaks of the stars, which he calls "thoughts of God in the heavens," or, in a childlike way, "the forget-me-nots of the angels"; whether he tells us of the thunders of the avalanche—those voices in which the mountains open their snowy lips to speak to each other in the primeval language; whether it is the magic moonlight on Louisiana's lakes, or the wild, wailing winter of the north, where the snow falls ever deeper, deeper, deeper—his soul is still the faithful mirror of nature, and it is the very spirit of the scenes he describes that breathes through him and touches us in his song.

And as his gentle sympathies go out toward nature, so do they lovingly twine around his human fellow-beings. He has the tenderest heart for children. Listen to these verses which he addresses to the little ones :

> " Ye open the eastern windows,
> That look towards the sun,
> Where thoughts are singing swallows
> And the brooks of morning run.

> " Ye are better than all the ballads
> That ever were sung or said ;
> For ye are living poems,
> And all the rest are dead."

He feels finely for little birds, as is shown by his beautiful poem on Walter von der Vogelweide, wherein he tells how the famous Minnesinger learned his art from the feathered songsters in the air, and out of gratitude made provision in his will that birds should always be fed on his tomb. He has a true sense of the miseries endured by the oppressed, as is shown by his beautiful poem on the Jewish Cemetery at Newport. But, above all, he expresses the noblest

American feeling for woman. And he has given us three ideal types of women, of which it is not too much to say that they are likely to become a heritage for our remote descendants : Evangeline, the type of woman's fidelity ; Elsie, the type of woman's self-sacrifice ; and the beautiful Minnehaha, the type of wifely fondness.

I have said that Longfellow is not a poet of the prophetic order. His poetry expresses certain general tender and noble feelings of the human heart. But the deepest regions of the heart he does not enter. The way into those regions lies through struggle and conflict. And struggle and conflict, inward as well as outward, the gentle poet shuns. Therefore the sublimest themes, the profoundest aspirations, of our time find no expression in his song. He soothes us, but he does not stir. Even when he sees great wrongs before him he never strikes the lyre in wrathful chords. The waves of his song do not rise high up against the beetling rocks of wrong ; they do but sob and moan upon the sands below. That such was the case we perceive in his poems on slavery. It was not in his nature to do battle. He appeals to Channing that he should " write and tell out this bloody tale." For his own part he sings of the slave's dream of liberty, or of the noble lady who liberated her slaves, or of the witnesses at the

bottom of the sea. He sympathizes keenly with the
sufferings of the oppressed, but he does not lend a
voice to the protest against the wrong of oppression,
or against the cruel oppressors. It is only in the
last of the series on slavery, in the "Warning," that
he rises for a moment to the height of prophecy in
speaking of the poor blind Samson of our land, the
negro, who may some day raise his hand against the
pillar of our commonwealth and make the vast temple of our liberty a shapeless mass of wreck and
rubbish.

But it is chiefly in one respect that we should regard Longfellow as a national poet. It is the mission of the poet to express the spirit of his age and
of his people. He must not utter only what he himself feels; then he will be no true poet. He must
say what all feel; then all will love him. Because
the poet expresses for us what moves all our hearts,
but what none of us can express so well as he, therefore our feelings find their satisfaction in pouring
through the channels which his verse has made.
And it is because Longfellow reflects in his poetry
the spirit of this people that he has come to be so
near and dear to the heart of the people. The spirit
of the American people is cosmopolitan. So is the
spirit of Longfellow's poetry cosmopolitan. We call
these United States the commingling place of all na-

tionalities, and we are proud to draw the elements
that make up our citizenship from every quarter of
the globe. So does Longfellow draw the elements
of his poetry from every clime and every time, bor-
rowing not only his themes, but also seeking to reproduce the feelings of distant lands and ages ; and
he invites the poets of all places and periods, as it
were, to an ideal citizenship on the American Par-
nassus. From the beginning of his career we see
him doing this, and he does not cease doing so
until the end. He goes to Spain to reproduce the
sombre martial spirit of the Spanish past, in the
funeral hymn of Manrique. He goes to Germany
for the inspiration of what is, perhaps, the finest
of his longer poems, the "Golden Legend"—a poem
ringing with the echoes of cloister bells, haunted by
visions of castles on the Rhine, and dim with the
dimness of cathedrals. He goes to France to revive
the songs of the Troubadours ; to Sweden and Nor-
way, to the land of the Vikings, and to far-off Asia.
And when he returns to his own America it is even
then not so much the life of the present or the an-
ticipation of the future that kindles his imagination,
but the old traditions, the oldest that such a young
American can offer—the legends of the Ojibways,
the traditions of the Puritans, and the touching tale
of love in an Acadian village, with thatched roofs

and dormer windows—which he rehearses in his flowing verses.

It is the Past that shines in the eyes of Longfellow. In him the spirit of America, ere it set out to create the glories of the future, has turned back once more to revisit, as in a dream, the mystic splendors of the past. There will come hereafter a grander America, a new national life, new attitudes of mind, new and original modes of feeling, new themes for action, new inspirations for song. And a mightier race of bards will then strike the lyre of America. But, however great the future may be, the people will never forget him who was the poet of their younger life, and of whom we may well say, using his own words concerning another, he was "a noble poet, one whose heart was like a nest of singing birds, rocked on the topmost bough of life." On the topmost bough of life, high up under the clear ether, in the golden light, hung the heart of Longfellow—that nest of song! To-day the nest is empty, the singing birds have flown away, but they have flown into the hearts of thousands, and are still singing there, and will go on singing for years and years to come, their sweet and purifying music.

LETTERS.

New York, April 8, 1882.

What impression would the work of Northern poets, as interpretative of ·Nature, make on a reader who had never seen the countries, or even the geographical zones, which they describe?

The question is a curious one. I may contribute something to it from my own experience.

I was born and brought up, until eighteen years old, in a tropical country that is exceptionally fortunate in its climate; winter or rough weather, in the sense of cold, there is none, "nor ever storm blows rudely," and though the snow lay visibly, nine days out of ten, upon the distant mountain-tops, it was through all my earlier years a mystery to me in its remoteness; and doubly tantalizing that I was eagerly reading, day by day, in my father's house by the seaside, of Northern winters and winter sports, of skating, snow-balling, sleighing, and striving to reconstruct in imagination the conditions of life in the fatherland. During these years the touch of

223

snow was unknown to me, while all the time the snow itself lay in sight upon the mountain summits. It was naturally to the poets' descriptions of winter and of autumn that I turned with especial interest. Bryant taught me what the American autumn was before I had seen its hectic in New England fields. Longfellow gave me most vivid impressions of winter. What pleasure it was to read and read again the "Midnight Mass for the Dying Year," "Woods in Winter," "Afternoon in February," and many a pictorial line or passage in the longer poems! In these I took an interest beyond their strictly poetical or imaginative charm—the interest, namely, of a mind seeking to find in those passages something literally interpretative of the alien outward nature which they described, some touch that should put before the inward eye the strange life which the bodily eye had not seen. I may say that the realization was fairly successful, though my efforts had to be supplemented by other writers than Longfellow, whose favorite season of the four was rather spring than winter, and who in none of his descriptions practised the extreme minuteness of realistic portraiture that was already becoming a common thing. Wordsworth has shown how unsafe the descriptions even of the professed apostles of Nature may be. In his poem on the "Influence of

Natural Objects," as it first appeared in "The Friend," he describes his sports on the ice; and he tells us that not seldom he left the tumultuous throng of his fellow-skaters

> " To cut across the image of a Star
> That gleamed upon the ice."

This is a flagrant example of scholastic athletics that have no counterpart in the possibilities of outward life. Longfellow dared less than Wordsworth in the minutely descriptive way, and consequently lies under the blame of fewer errors of commission. But the positive data which the tropical reader found in his poetry for the reconstruction of the North, with its ice and fogs and tempests, though they were valuable, were not abundant. One thing which the Northern poets might have described for the Southern reader, but inexcusably did not describe, was frozen snow—snow that has been softened and recongealed; and I shall never forget the disappointment caused me by this culpable neglect on the part of the various poets of Nature whom I had read. For when at last, grown to an active boy, I climbed the summit of Mauna Kea to touch the wondrous snow that I had gazed on so long, I found it no fleecy substance, no pile of plastic flakes, but on the contrary a rigid mass of crystals that refused to yield to my touch, and clung as stubbornly to the ground as if they were a part of the lava-bed on which they rested. It was a surprise for which I blamed the poets.

Still the poets were full of help for the reconstruction of the Northern seasons. When first I saw falling 'snow (I remember it was in the college grounds at New Haven) it seemed a thing familiar enough, and I was glad of this, fearing to be scoffed at for my ignorance. But as none of my companions seemed to suspect it, I confessed to one of them that this was my first snow-storm ; and learned that it was well not to be too frank, as he instantly proposed a sound snow-balling as the correct treatment of the stranger from the tropics. Longfellow's poems had not prepared me for this reception.

TITUS MUNSON COAN.

•

6 EAST FOURTEENTH STREET, NEW YORK,
April 10, 1882.

The death of Henry Wadsworth Longfellow reminds me once more of some of the pleasantes hours of my youth, and of the evidence of the wide diffusion of his writings as far back as 1853. I was then fresh from my first enthusiasm in poetry, having read "Rokeby" with the pleasure that one takes when he enters a new and beautiful land, and eagerly looks forward to the pleasure he anticipates from continued pursuit of its unexplored attractions. Living then on the enchanting shores of the Bosphorus, at the village of Bebek, in the suburbs of Constantinople, where every prospect suggested some historic legend, and every glimpse of the scenery fired the imagination; where the climate is of the softest, the landscape hued in the most vivid tints, the people picturesque to the last degree, the nightingale's song pervading the still, moonlit watches of the night, and life steeped in an atmosphere of romance, there could have been no poetry better qualified to please the ardor of a youth spent in that spot than the cantos of "Rokeby," the strophes of "Childe Harold," and the pathetic cadences of "Evangeline," or the stately measures of "Nuremberg" and the "Belfry of Bruges." •

Already were the poems of Longfellow familiar to the English and American residents at the Turkish capital, and even to some of the better educated of the Greek population, through the choice little volumes bearing the imprimatur of Ticknor & Fields, and bound in brown cloth stamped with a design which is well known to all who are familiar with

American poetry. At the delightful little waterside hamlet of Bebek we English-speaking boys had formed a small literary club, where we recited the poems of Longfellow, while in our idle hours he was one of our favorites. I well remember often sitting in a certain window overlooking the Bosphorus, watching or sketching the fleets slowly dropping down the azure current from the Black Sea ; nearer by gleamed the gilded spire of the minaret above the grove of chenars beneath whose shade the Turk enjoyed his nargile, and beyond arose the pointed roof of the sultan's pavilion in the Valley of Heavenly Waters. There we read and reread the admirable translation of Jasmin's "Blind Girl of Castel Cuillé," and discussed or learned by heart the thrilling lines of "Excelsior," or passages from the romance of the heroine of Acadie. The melodious descriptions of American scenery filled us with longings to see the great continent beyond the sea, or the "Wreck of the Schooner Hesperus" thrilled the imagination like a touch of winter and storm suddenly infused into the amenity of the scene upon which we were gazing. An English youth, one of the brightest of our number, was for ever reciting verses from Byron's "Isles of Greece" or Longfellow's "Excelsior." About that time also a cloud which for a while threw its shadow over the noonday of our happiness gave peculiar significance to the "Voices of the Night" and "Resignation"—a poem which has probably contributed more to console the sorrowing than any other poem of its length in the language.

Was it a small thing that the dead poet should have diffused so widely the influence of his genius, helping to shape character in other lands, to ennoble the heart, to inspire just sentiments of life, and encourage the inexperienced or the afflicted with songs of hope and cheer? With the ever-increasing advance of foreign influences and education in the East it may be safely predicted that the poems of Longfellow are destined to be more widely read and appreciated there for many years to come.

S. G. W. BENJAMIN.

THE STUDIO, NEW YORK, April 15, 1882.

MY DEAR MR. STODDARD: Ever since my visit to Cambridge to make drawings for your article in *Scribner* I have felt glad to have had such an opportunity to know the peculiarly gentle and considerate qualities of mind and heart that characterized Mr. Longfellow.

On presenting your letter of introduction, making

known the object of my visit to Cambridge, he received me most cordially, and gave me every opportunity to do my work.

His life appeared to be a very busy one, consequently I took particular pains not to disturb him.
He quickly perceived this feeling, and would look me
up two or three times a day, somewhere about the
grounds or in some part of the house, wherever I
happened to be.   He said one day : "A plate was
placed for you at the table yesterday, but when the
dinner-hour came I looked for you where I had seen
you a moment before, and you were not to be found.
You reminded me of a Prince Rupert's drop."

One lovely, sunny morning, while I was sketching in the rear of the house, sounds of a voice singing, accompanied by a piano, came to me through an
open window.   Presently Mr. Longfellow came out
and asked me to go in and hear the singing, saying a
lady friend had called and that she sang so finely he
could not let her go without hearing her sing, and
that he believed I, too, would.enjoy it.

The singing was admirable, and song after song
was called for.   Mr. Longfellow's face expressed the
great pleasure he felt.   After the music he talked of
places and associations vividly recalled by the music.

On another occasion the conversation drifted upon
the immortality of the soul and the future life.   He

spoke with great feeling, and expressed a firm belief that we should preserve our identity and that we should meet our old and loved friends.

He left upon my mind a strong impression that his life had been spent in a world quite different from the common, and that the beauty of his character had in great part created it.

Very truly your friend,

R. SWAIN GIFFORD.

CONCORD, MASS., April 24, 1882.

MY DEAR STODDARD: It is nearly twenty years since I saw Mr. Longfellow. At that time I was a boy in school or college, and he had for me the interest of a handsome historical subject chiefly—an object whose name was Longfellow, and who had written most of the poetry with which at that period I was familiar. But, as you know, he and my father were college friends, and as long as our household held together he was a household word with us. He was among the first to speak up about "Twice-Told Tales." And, on the other hand, my mother used to tell us that my father made him a present of "Evangeline"; for, the two being in talk together, Hawthorne alluded to the theme as one that he might possibly use in a story, and Longfellow thereupon evinced such a hearty appreciation of the poetical potentialities of it that Hawthorne finally said, with a smile, " Well, it belongs to you," or words to that effect. I remember reading to my father a few months before he died the passage in " Evangeline " which describes her discovery of her lover in the hospital, and his death. He listened with a certain profound and still attention that sometimes characterized him, and at the end seemed inwardly and quietly moved. My mother, who probably had some presentiment even then that her own grief might not be far distant, said to me afterwards, half reproachfully : " Why did you read papa that ? " But perhaps it was as fit a word as any other for the time.

How much or often my father used to read Longfellow I know not ; but he used to encourage or urge me to learn many of his poems by heart, stimulating my appetite thereto by first reading them aloud to me himself and giving ear afterwards to my declamations of them, which were apt to take place during our walks through fields and woods. " The Skeleton in Armor " was one of my first and best-loved acquisitions in this kind, and the first "piece" I spoke at school was the passage in " The Building of the Ship " beginning "Thou, too, sail on, O Ship of State!" which my father selected for me, and which (this was

in 1861) doubtless had for him a sufficiently grave
and earnest significance, the Ship being then under
much stress of weather. "Hiawatha   had appeared
previously, while we were still in England, and my
father chuckled over some parts of it ; but on the
whole I think he admired it as much as anything
that Longfellow wrote, and returned to it oftener.

When my father died Longfellow came to the
funeral, and I saw him standing at the open grave
with his hat off, the sunshine falling on his gray hair.
A week or two afterwards he wrote to my mother en-
closing the first draft of the eloquent little poem that
ends, you remember,

> " Ah! who shall lift that wand of magic power,
>   Or the lost clew regain?
>   The unfinished window in Aladdin's tower
>   Unfinished must remain "

—true poetry, and truth, too, if there ever was any.
The letter itself was very beautiful and kind, and if I
knew where it was I would send it to you.   Possibly
it may have been published already, for all New England seems to have taken to writing Longfellow's biography.

Another little poem of his, about the battle in
Hampton Roads between the *Merrimac* and the
Cumberland, was read to my father and me by James

T. Fields before its publication in the *Atlantic*. Mr.
Fields read with good emphasis and discretion, and
my father expressed a strong liking for the poem,
which likewise had the distinction of being declaimed
by me the following Wednesday at school, much to
Mr. Sanborn's edification, he not having, of course,
heard it before.

This pretty nearly exhausts my available reminiscences of Longfellow. They resemble those of every
one else who was brought into any kind of relations
with him, in being wholly pleasant. It was easy to
comprehend that gracious and gentle character, and
impossible not to love him, at least as far as one's
comprehension went. He died a few days after my
return from a ten years' visit to Europe, so that I had
no opportunity to supplement my boyish by any ma-
turer knowledge of him. Many famous men are leaving us nowadays, but none, perhaps, has been so
generally mourned ; and it is certainly much to the
general credit that this should be so.

Yours very sincerely,

JULIAN HAWTHORNE.

BOSTON PUBLIC LIBRARY, May 5, 1882.

MY DEAR STODDARD: I have delayed answering
your letter because I did not know what to say ; nor

do I now, only this : A thousand words, or ten thousand, might be written about "some uncollected poems of Longfellow." There are, as you well know, a dozen or more which were printed in his college days, of which only four or five were published in his collected writings as "earlier poems."

A reference to these, with a few lines and stanzas culled from them here and there as specimens, might be prefaced by an account of the circumstances under which they were published in the *United States Literary Gazette.* This *Gazette* has a history not without interest; for among the contributors to its first volumes, contemporaneously with the Longfellow boy, were Bryant, Percival, Grenville Mellen, etc., etc., all of which you know, and more too.

In a letter in my collection, written to the editor, Longfellow aspired to be associate editor of the journal; and from this some extracts might be made. You see the nature of the materials which might be worked up into a readable chapter by "a literary feller" who has a light hand and deft touch for such matters, the which I neither am nor have.

Very truly yours,
MELLEN CHAMBERLAIN.

THE CENTURY, NEW YORK, May 8, 1861.

MY DEAR STODDARD: You ask me to tell you
what I may know of Mr. Longfellow. I wish I
could say I knew him; yet the little I saw of him—
only twice—made me seem at least to know the
genial, kindly, true poetic nature of the man. I met
him first at the University Press, in Cambridge, and
was introduced to him by my friend, that most
capable of printers, Mr. Welch. Mr. Longfellow
seemed to know something of me, greeted me very
cordially, and asked me to walk up with him to his
house. I had the pleasure of doing so and of talk-
ing an hour with him, he inquiring of many English
matters, among others, I recollect, of the poems of
my old friend, W. B. Scott. Need I say it was a
pleasant hour, memorable, though I do not pretend
to repeat anything he said? This must have been ten
years ago. Some two years ago I ventured to call
again to introduce the editor of the *American Art
Review*, Mr. Koehler, we wanting some authorization
or aid from Mr. Longfellow in order to obtain per-
mission to copy a certain portrait. Mr. Longfellow
himself opened the door to us, and on my asking if
he recollected me, answered graciously that he did,
and took us into his sitting-room. Our visit being
really on business, we did not feel justified in pro-

longing it, though certainly we were not hurried off;
and again I recall the pleasantness of a most informal and kindly reception. This is nothing to tell
you, but it is much for me to recollect.   I saw and
spoke with him—that was enough.

W. J. LINTON.

ASTOR LIBRARY, NEW YORK, May 8, 1882.

Among the cherished memories of distinguished
men of letters, in both hemispheres, it has been my
privilege to have met, not the least interesting is that
of Professor Longfellow.   Some few summers since,
when visiting the "modern Athens of America,"
and in company with a clerical friend from Newton,
we drove to the classic town of Cambridge, so re-
nowned for its halls of learning and its picturesque
beauties, both of nature and art.   We called at the
Craigie House to pay our respects to Mr. Longfellow,
and we were not only so fortunate as to find him at
leisure, but he received us with such courteous ur-
banity and unostentatious kindness as at once made
us feel at ease in his presence, and led to a very
interesting conversation concerning literature and
literary men, his travels in Europe, etc.

Not having noted down any memoranda of these
items, many, or most of them, have now escaped my
memory; and yet, now that he has passed away,

even fragments of his wise words possess for us a value unknown before. His generous, and even enthusiastic, praise of the works of several of his brother bards was conspicuous, as illustrative of his native modesty—the modesty of true genius. In this respect he not only resembled Washington Irving, but also no less in his kindliness of nature and gentle courtesy of deportment. As we entered the historic home of the poet the first object that met our gaze was the quaint "old clock on the stairs," and, passing into the drawing-room, we were cordially received by the host, although my acquaintance with him had hitherto been merely by correspondence. This reception-room was decked and garnished with great artistic taste, the walls being covered with choice paintings and portraits, while the bookcases were surmounted with statuary, and the tables loaded with valuable relics and objects of *virtu* and *bijouterie*. In fine, this presence-chamber looked like a combination of a poet's pleasaunce and an artist's studio. In course of our gossip, having referred to the great popularity of Mr. Ruskin in England, and also in the United States, as an authority in the department of Art Criticism, Mr. Longfellow replied: "He resembles a squadron of cavalry sweeping all before them and taking the field. Ruskin is a master of style," he continued, "and, although not wholly unimpeachable, he is usually correct." When the names were mentioned of James Russell Lowell, the author of the "Autocrat of the Break-fast-Table," and Whittier, he did not fail to recognize and applaud their distinctive and characteristic merits. And yet more earnestly did he accord to Ralph Waldo Emerson his high meed of fame. It was our good fortune to visit the philosopher on the following day, and to listen to his sententious wisdom for a brief, delightful hour. Mr. Longfellow took us through his several apartments and into sundry nooks and corners, in which many a precious tome was carefully treasured and "kept from eyes profane." When travelling in Italy, he said, he found an incomplete set of Bodoni's celebrated edition of Dante ; it lacked but one volume, yet, imperfect as it was, it was too great a prize to be lost or left behind, so he brought the volumes home with him, never expecting to find the missing one. To his joyful surprise, however, he found it, some months after his return home, at a bookstall in an obscure street of Boston. His eye lighted up with evident pleasure and pride as he exhibited to us the now complete set of this dainty edition of Dante. Just as we were about to take our leave he referred to the splendidly illustrated edition, in two volumes quarto, of his Complete Works, and expressed his unqualified pleasure and satisfaction at the rare beauty of the designs and the typography. He also mentioned the fact that such was the scarcity of the first edition of his poems that a copy had been offered for sale at five hundred dollars. The home of Professor Longfellow—which has been often described by the pen and portrayed by the pencil—like the quaint, picturesque Cottage at Sunnyside, and that of the Sage of Concord, is so well known to the lovers of elegant literature and poesy that hereafter many pilgrim feet will wend their way thither, as to the "Meccas of the mind," to pay their tribute of grateful regard. And for myself, never shall the delightful episode of a summer vacation be lost to memory that brought me face to face, for a brief interval, with one of the most gifted and genial of men I have ever met; and, if I may cite the words of an eminent English author and tourist who shared the like pleasure, I would add, "Nor shall I ever forget that I have been permitted to touch the hand and to listen to the discourse, full of calm, and wise, and gentle things, of a noble American gentleman—of him who wrote the 'Psalm of Life,' 'The Village Blacksmith,' and 'Evangeline'; of him whose life has been blameless, whose record is pure, whose name is a sound of fame to all people." FREDERICK SAUNDERS.

HENRY WADSWORTH LONGFELLOW.

(AN IMPROVISATION.)

THE clamorous, sorrowful bells
Are swinging out their knells.

THE BELLS.

Defunctos ploro!
Pestem fugo!
Festa decoro!

Floating under heaven's wide arch,
Along on the boisterous winds of March.
Over the multitudinous street,
Where, hushed with awe, the mourners meet,
Are flinging about their knells,
As when the great organ sinks and swells.

THE BELLS.

Funera plango!
Fulgura frango!
Sabbata pango!

Winging their ghostly way above,
Like the snow-white Pentecostal Dove;
Singing the being just begun:
This is my well-beloved son,

On his journey to Paradise,
With its light in his eyes;
Saying: "*Benedictus qui venis;*
Manibus o date lilia plenis";
Passing the houses, hung with black,
As though the world was a-wrack;
Passing the hearses, with nodding plumes,
Sable as night; passing the tombs,
     Daily and nightly
     Gleaming whitely,
As when March snoweth,
He cometh and goeth.

THE BELLS.

Laudo Deum verum!
Congrego clerum!

Who are those that come on the Atlantic waves to the west-
     ward,
Crossing in low, little vessels, a fair-haired Germanic people,
Masters of horses and steers, the wit of the wise and wary,
Masters, and stalwart of arm, that know not to be down-
     trodden?
These are the sons of the meadows of Yorkshire, sons of the
     Aldens.
Summers two hundred and thirty departed in old-fashioned
     England
Since the first of these comers, stout William, was christened
     Longfellow.
William crossed over in youth with others, and landed elated.

Soon was he happily wed to a maiden, his neighbor, Anne
 Sewall.
William and Anne ere long were the parents—for they were
 prolific—
Who knows of how many children, with grandchildren—last of
 all Stephen,
Sire of the sweet singer, Henry, who late, to our sorrow, de-
 parted.
Such was the birth and such were the parents of Longfellow,
 Poet.

> Duly in the morning,
> With his satchel in his hands,
> Childe Henry hastened schoolward
> And into faery lands:
> A studious youth who conned his books,
> Which were to him like wayside brooks
> That sparkled
> And darkled
> As is the look of country streams
> To wee, wee boys in summer dreams—
> Such as our young master,
> All alive,
> Like a bee in his hive,
> Singing faster and faster.
>
> When twice the teens came round him
> The rooms of Bowdoin bound him:
> There with many a college-mate,
> Some of them jocund, some sedate,
> One of them famous, another great.

Mighty was Captain Nathaniel,
Whose father was lost at sea ;
With the insight of Hebrew Daniel,
Seer of men was he,
And will be ever, the world now knows ;
Sharp as the hawthorn, sweet as the rose.
They studied shelves of learned tomes,
Both in and out of season—
Georgeous Cheever who chose the Church,
And the Abbott of Unreason.
What is the ditty that Hawthorne sings,
Like a little robin that prunes its wings ?
" *We are beneath the dark blue sky,*
   And the moon is shining bright ;
Oh ! what can lift the soul so high
   As the glow of a summer night,
When all the gay are hushed to sleep,
And they that mourn forget to weep,
   Beneath that gentle light ? "

And what is the song that Henricus sings,
Like an angel that spreads his new-come wings ?
He chants the hymns that he hears at Church
To the drone of the dull precentor,
Who sometimes leaves the choir in the lurch,
A sorry sort of Mentor ;
Dirges for dead folk, lauds for the living,
And evermore Thanksgiving,
Then to the tinkle of light guitars,
Under Venetian moon and stars,

He trills, where gondolas glide,
·His donna by his side.
" Fair Juliet ! oh ! ease the woe
Of your heart-breaking Romeo ;
O Rosaline! be love of mine,
For my sick soul doth peak and pine.
Marino ! no, it must not be ;
Fly for your life, O Foscari !
Or the Doges will cease to wed the sea !
The Bucentaur will nevermore
Put proudly from old Adria's shore ;
For note, a Shadow mounting stark
Upon the Wing'd Steed of St. Mark !
Whence doth that fearful cry arise ?
What dark Shape crosses the Bridge of Sighs ?
The Council of Ten are One—
The deed of death will be done."

The pupil becomes Professor
Of Languages and Letters ;
Able they knew at twenty-two
To teach his elders—not betters ;
For better than poets none can be,
So their hearts are high and their souls are free.
Imagine where our Professor went,
Seeking the clerkly Continent ;
Over the sunk Atlantides ;
Between the Pillars of Hercules ;
Past Calpe, and the Afric shore,
Where Hanno sailed in days of yore,

Dipping his weary oar
From Nothing into the Nevermore—
For Carthage is fall'n, and Hannibal
Has gone—great hero—the way of all!
Conceive the course our Pilot steered,
The coasts that appeared and disappeared,
The mirror of blue
His bark went through,
The mountains that rose and sunk again,
The firmament and the under-plain;
Hither and thither, as sea-birds wheel,
Pushes his prow and glides his keel;
Jason reaching the Golden Fleece,
And the Isle of the Hesperides,
Where the guarded apples are rosy mellow,
And drop in the hands of this good fellow:
Evoe Bacchus! Io Pæan!
Over the waves of the glad Ægean!

(LONGFELLOW VATES LOQUITUR.)

" Genius of Petrarch! guide my willing pen,
While I essay therewith an amorous lay,
Such as thou shapedst for Laura—well-a-day,
Priest as thou wert, thou hadst the lover's ken;
So had thy greater, Dante, man of men,
For grimly daring in the downward way,
To the Inferno, whence its punished may
Perchance emerge—oh! tell us, Vergil, when ?
A nun my spirit hath perceived in dreams,
Like her whom Milton saw through Cambridge trees,

What time he slumbered by the reedy shore
Of Camus, lucidest of poetic streams,
Sacred to chaste Sabrina, couched at ease
On sliding waves that waft her back no more.

Lordlings, will ye hear me tell,
If I can, of poor Rudel?
How the dreamer lived to reach
The far Tripolitan beach,
Though he was deprived of speech;
How the Countess, as was meet,
Kissed him, dying at her feet?
Or is Pierre Vidal your friend,
Who of Troubadours was first,
Who celebrated each diurna,
Now Le Louve and now Na Vierna,
Fond and fickle to the end?
No; a manlier strain be mine:
True love, losing, does not whine;
Such a gracious strain was thine,
Masterful Poet, most Divine!

Shut here at Bankside by the loathèd stage,
My fancy wanders through Verona's streets,
Where by the moonlight in unnatural rage
Rash Romeo, reft of reason, Tybalt meets;
So would not I my lover, who I know
Doth much abuse my poor, confiding faith.
Wild Heart! why trample on thy vassal so,
Strange Rose of Beauty, who arts till my scathe?

Can no two men be true when comes between
Their twin-dear souls a woman—fiend, I say,
For such is she, my bane, that is thy Queen,
Poor Marlowe's fatal Hero, born to slay.
      But her I love no longer; stronger far
      Over me rises now a western star.

The Phosphor Nun sets slowly where I am,
Behind these dim old wharves of Rotterdam;
But Hesper floateth hither, for she sees
I yearn for the rich dusk of Cambridge trees,
The shadows of my immemorial elms,
Wherethrough a sunset glory overwhelms
The life that is, foretelling that to be,
When she I love bethinks her to love me;
And from our heaven-made marriage nuptial joys
Shall bourgeon into beauteous girls and boys,
Whose tiny feet, that creep in unawares,
Tick with the half-heard Clock upon the stairs,
Under the roof that sheltered One
Who was the New World's noblest son,
Fatherless father of generations,
Which will break into sorest lamentations
When he, who is as strong as just,
Sinks down, as all must sink, to dust;
Going down, as I—I see my going—
Not when June winds but March are blowing,
Done to death, but not afraid.
Who made will care for what He made.

Rapt in a wind of prophecy
(Or does a Presence speak through me ?)

I know to-day what I shall be.
Not of myself—I am but lent,
To Something a ready instrument,
Subject to that, as to winds the lute,
Powerless the high gods to salute—
Nothing, but *all* when breathed upon
By the awful mouth of the Unseen One!
Therefore I say that I shall teach
Thousands in sinewy Saxon speech,
Out of French, German, and Spanish
Recall what the ages strove to banish:
Chansons as light as a humming-bird's wing;
A song of sorrow a seraph might sing
(" *Yo el Re!* " doth Death repeat
To Don Jorge in the skirmish near Cañavete);
The three Worlds of the Florentine,
Whose soul re-risen hath entered mine;
A Danish stave, where cannon roar;
A tavern-ballad of Elsinore,
Trolled in the castle where Hamlet dwells,
Where the jester Yorick jangles his bells;
A quiet alehouse on the Rhine,
Where I with other old comrades dine,
Burschen all, and dozens of *stein*,
(There is no harm in this good wine);
Lays such as Michael Drayton sang,
Whose lines like swords upon armor rang;
Homeric hexameters restored
To honor the Supper of our Lord;
Calderon, a little *sub rosa*,
To glance at the dancing of Preciosa ;

Belgic *carillons* (none can be purer);
The Nuremberg of Albrecht Dürer;
A-building of ships, and sailor lore;
The lost playmate that comes no more;
Indian Eddas, old as the leaves
That whirl through their woods on autumn eves;
Spirits of bird and beast at one,
Human as we, when all is done;
The elements in their natural shapes,
What pursues and what escapes;
Runic sages, rough and wrong;
Tartar, mayhap, and Turkman song;
A Golden Legend, not beat out thin;
A hundred Tales of a Wayside Inn;
Rabbis, musicians, scientists, doctors,
Very reverend dons and proctors;
There will be no end to the songs I sing,
Till the cold hand shatters my string.
Then the world will own it has missed us,
When we quit it like Trismegistus!
These make me beloved in a hundred lands,
And give me the grasp of a million hands,
The friendship of man, woman, child,
Who are to mortality reconciled.
Poets will love me, peoples crown—
With one only sorrow that will not down;
Darkly it looms like a funeral pyre
Where what was woman is lapped in fire!
Jesu merci! But no, if it must,
Let the heavens fall, we know Whom to trust.
The end will come when my beard is white,

Will suddenly come in a still March night.
For hark! I hear—they are drawing near—
The clamorous, sorrowful bells
Wherewith Mount Auburn tells
That a singer has crossed its portals
And joined the immortals.
The holy Mount Auburn bells
Are pealing their farewell knells."

THE BELLS.

Funera plango!
Fulgura frango!
Sabbata pango!
Kyrie eleison!
Christe eleison!

Passion Sunday, March 25-26, 1882.

THE END.

www.ingramcontent.com/pod-product-compliance
Lightning Source LLC
Chambersburg PA
CBHW020351030726

47496CB00007B/2094